The Navajo Woman
A Western Novel

Richard G. Hole

Far West

SYNOPSIS

They had reached the road.

The horses followed him. The path widened, and it seemed that the gorge to their left was getting shallower.

Trees partly covered it.

The path widened still further, forming a kind of platform, with the wall leaning over it in a kind of visor.

And there, in the grass, was a body.

He was stretched out on the ground, on his side.

She wore a fringed-edged suede skirt high above tan legs.

Two turned arms, the same hazel color, covered the head.

The Navajo Woman is a story belonging to the Far West Collection, a collection of novels developed in the American Wild West.

THE NAVAJO WOMAN

CHAPTER I

The road steepened in the last few meters and soon after disappeared. To the right, a rocky wall. To the left, a cliff.

"Are you sure you haven't taken the wrong turn, Mac?

Mac shook his head. He was a man in his forties, with red hair and beard. He was wearing very worn clothes.

"No, what happens is that there was a landslide. You have to skip that and the path continues further. Clay ...

"What happen?

"Gold is close.

"Well.

Mac looked at him from under the brim of his hat.

"You don't seem very enthusiastic. Well, the truth is, you hardly get excited about anything.

Clay didn't reply. He was probably ten years younger than his partner and clean-shaven. His black hair fell in a peak over his forehead. He had removed his hat and was letting the mountain air dry his sweat.

"Okay, shall we?

"Yes," Clay said.

His clothes, though dusty, looked in better shape than Mac's. His hands were gloved.

They spurred the horses and they rushed to the assault of the mound. Their horseshoes slipped on the hard earth, but they finally managed to crown him. From above, the cliff looked terrifying. In the distance, clouds were gathering, blocking out the setting sun.

"Do you see the way? Down there.

"I see.

"We will make the night a little further. There is a cave. I remember perfectly, although it was two years since I was here, the last time.

He turned to his partner.

"Listen, friend. When we have the gold ...

"We will talk when we have the gold.

"Okay, okay. I just wanted to tell you that we will part ways in town. We agreed to that, right?

"If we are already at that, why talk more?

Then suddenly Clay slapped his partner on the shoulder.

"Mac, if I don't speak, it's because I don't feel like talking. But it's nothing personal against you.

"I know. But sometimes I think that a man is relieved if a weight is lifted off his shoulders. I've spent a lot of time alone and I know it.

"Well, in that case, with a devil, shut up and let's follow the path. We'll part ways or not, anyone knows, but I'll tell you one thing, Mac: I couldn't have chosen a better partner.

"I suppose I should feel very happy about those words and dance a jig, but damn, even though you are the closest thing to a dead man, it seems to me that I could not have found a better travel companion either. And here we are talking nonsense, when the night is creeping up on us.

They had reached the road. The horses followed him. The path widened, and it seemed that the gorge to their left was getting shallower. Trees partly covered it.

The wall, to the right, formed a promontory. Mac folded it first. When Clay caught up with him, he heard his partner exclaim and saw him standing.

"What the hell is going on?

"Look at that, Clay" said the other, in a low voice.

The path widened still further, forming a kind of platform, with the wall leaning over it in a kind of visor.

And there, in the grass, was a body.

He was stretched out on the ground, on his side. Clay saw a suede skirt, fringed at the edge, high above tan legs. Two turned arms, the same hazel color, covered the head.

"A woman," Clay said, dismounting.

"It must have fallen from up there," Mac replied.

They were already next to the body. Clay shook it and a face, framed by two black braids, came into view.

"An Indian," Mac said, frowning.

Clay lowered his eyes to his legs. Then, with a brusque movement, he put his hand on the woman's chest.

"She's alive," he said after a moment. Come on, help me.

He took the body in his arms and stood up. The woman had her eyes closed. He was young and his face had a strange, whitish hue.

"Hell," said Mac. Hell, I think ...

"Shut up and help me.

He placed it on the horse's neck. Carefully, as I could with a creature.

"How far away is that cave you told me about?

"Oh hell, less than five hundred yards.

"Is there water there?

"Yes, by the way there is. Clay, that woman ...

"Shut up. Go.

Leading the horse by the reins, he began to walk. Mac mounted and herded the mules.

The Indian woman stirred. Clay put his hand on her bare shoulder. The soft leather blouse, dyed in colors, was torn.

They did not speak until they reached the cave. It was big and spacious; it showed its mouth adorned with bulrush.

"Bring water and light the fire.

"Clay ...

"I said do it, damn it. Wait, I'll light the fire while you bring the water.

He carefully laid the Indian woman's body on the dry sand of the cave. She opened her eyes and a look of horror appeared in them. He made a move to sit up.

"Hold it, little girl," said Clay. Quiet. Be still.

She didn't seem to hear him. He rolled his eyes and his body stiffened.

Clay held her gently, but firmly.

"Quiet, come on, little one, quiet.

Mac returned with the water in the skins. He gave them a curious look and poured the water into the kettle.

"Quick," Clay said. Fast. And you, be still. Mac, you know a lot about Indians. Do you know which tribe this may be from?

He held her by both shoulders. She had closed her eyes and her body relaxed. He seemed to have lost consciousness again.

"She is a Navajo. Look at those pictures on the skirt.

"Can you speak to him in his language?

"I can, if she's not dead or ...

"It is not. Come on, let's light the fire.

Ten minutes later, the water was almost boiling. Clay walked to his mule and took out a leather saddlebag.

"What the hell are you going to do? Asked Mac.

Clay straightened up.

"Mac, you've seen the same thing as me, right?

"Yes I think so.

"Something has happened to that woman, and I imagine what it is.

His teeth were clenched. His face was pale.

"But you, what the hell can you do?

Clay had opened the saddlebag. From it he took out a wallet.

Mac leaned over him.

"But that... is that yours?

"It's mine. Put some water in a clean pot.

"But...

Clay faced him.

"You have not understood me? Will I have to do it all?

"No, Clay, hell. I like it as little as you do, but I will help you.

Clay returned to the young woman. The sun had set behind a dense mass of clouds.

"There will be a storm soon," Mac said.

"I'm going to heal her," Clay said.

Mac looked away.

"Damn" he said. Curse. I have seen many things, but "that" has always ...

"Have you also seen women raped? Clay asked dryly.

His hands maneuvered deftly and safely.

"He's coming to, Mac. Hold his arms.

The Indian woman opened her mouth, but no sound came from her lips. However, his entire shocked face was that of a person who "is screaming."

"With a devil ...

Mac held her arms. The body writhed.

Speak to him on his tongue or punch him on the jaw.

Mac began to speak. The Indian woman turned her face toward him, her expression strange. Mac continued to speak to her slowly, while holding her arms. Then she suddenly stopped resisting, but her mouth remained open.

Clay finished. He took a blanket and spread it over the girl's body. Then he rummaged through his suitcase and turned to Mac.

Tell him I'm going to give him medicine. That will take away the pain.

Mac spoke. She seemed to listen to him. He shook his head and opened his mouth. Then, Clay spilled a few drops on his tongue. He took the head in his hands and examined the back of her neck. I was there. A wound with dried blood. He washed it and examined it.

"It doesn't seem too bad," he said. This is what caused him to lose consciousness.

"I'd like," said Mac, slowly, chewing on the words, "take the scoundrel who did this and chat with him for half an hour. Chat and do some things to him that I know too.

Clay was on his feet. He washed his hands in the hot water. He turned to his partner.

"And I would like to witness it" he said.

The Indian woman had closed her eyes. It seemed to sleep.

"What have you given him?

"Opium.

Mac pulled out the rubber bag where he kept his tobacco. He began to roll a cigarette with shaking hands.

"Clay, you... all those tools... and you have opium. Your...

"I am, Mac, don't worry. I am a doctor.

"Yes, you are, hell. You are. One need only see what you have done for that poor creature.

Clay had turned his back on Mac.

"I think we should make dinner," he said.

"What I don't understand is that ...

"Shut up, would you?

"Yes.

Mac started making dinner. He watched as Clay put his hand on the Indian woman's forehead and then felt her pulse.

"Is very bad?

"He has a slight fever. Mac, what is the closest town?

"Last, and it's not close. It's fifty miles.

"You have to take it somewhere. If it gets worse, I couldn't do much here.

"There is the Dulles post. Twenty miles down that hill. On the road.

"Mac.

"Yes?

"Would you mind...?

"Hell no, Clay. It should be done. Gold can wait. They are not going to take it away.

"You are a good guy, Mac.

"Go to hell. Who could have been ... the cursed pig that did that to him?

"An Indian?

"Could be, Clay. There are Indians and whites who deserve to be hanged.

"Mac, she understood you.

"It seems so, but he has not responded. Maybe he speaks another dialect, but those pictures are Navajo.

"It's not that, Mac. Haven't you noticed? It is mute.

Damn it, Clay.

"I can not speak. Probably never has. She wanted to scream, but she can't. But she is not deaf. He calmed down when you spoke to him.

"I told her that you were going to cure her and that we would not do anything wrong to her. I repeated it to him.

"Yes.

There was a silence.

The sharp smell of fried bacon rose from the skillet.

"Let's have dinner. I'll put the coffee.

"Yeah come on.

* * *

The next morning, the sun was not visible, hidden behind the clouds. In the distance thunder sounded.

Clay approached the Indian woman. This one had her eyes open. He took her pulse.

An expression of relief appeared on his face.

"No fever, Mac.

Mac handed him a can of coffee.

"Tell her that I am going to heal her again. Reassure her if you can.

Her eyes were wide. He hardly moved.

"So, what can we do now? It's better?

"Seems. Mac, stay with her for a bit. I'm going back to where it happened. Maybe there is something there.

It took him no more than an hour to return.

"I have not found anything. Maybe you ...

"I will look at it. But...

A thick drop fell on his hand. Then another. More. They entered the cave.

"That will erase all tracks, Clay. I think it would be useless. I should have gone.

"Well, the damage is done.

It rained all morning. And at noon, the weather was still gray and cold.

They ate, and gave the Indian woman food. She kept looking at them, but there was no longer fear in her eyes. It was then that Clay said:

"Mac, try it.

"What?

"There must be some way for him to tell us who it was.

But, Clay, he can't speak.

"I know.

He frowned.

"We are fucking assholes, right, Mac?

"I don't even know what you're talking about.

"Here, guys, while there's gold around, huh? Waiting for us to arrive to pick it up. And we, here, next to that savage.

Mac stood up.

"Clay, if there were sun I'd tell you you've had too much. What the hell are you saying?

"I say we are fucking idiots.

"And I say... Damn you bastard, if that's what you think!...

Clay smiled.

"I just wanted to test you, Mac. Under those beards and under that filthy shirt is a man.

Mac dropped again.

"How, Clay? How can we do it?

"I do not know...

He frowned.

"Mac, the Indians paint. And all his paintings have a meaning. Water, earth, sky, distances ... His drawings are ideographic.

"I do not understand that last, but they do paint.

"She can do it, Mac. Maybe.

Mac rolled a cigarette.

"I'll try.

He bent over the Indian and began to speak to her. Slowly, in monosyllables. She gazed at him with her eyes, surrounded by long black lashes. Beneath the smooth forehead, what thoughts could be unrolling? Clay was staring at her. She had been able to see the perfect body hidden in the suede skirt and blouse. The Indian women are not usually beautiful, but this was a good sample of their race.

Then she suddenly took a hand out of the shroud. With a stiff finger, he pointed to the fire. Then he waved his hand in the air.

"Mac, give him a brand," Clay said. Maybe that's what you want.

Mac showed India a dull brand. She reached out her hand to him.

He took it by the unburned part. Clay got to his feet, picked up a smoothed stone, and set it next to the girl.

The hand dropped. She sat up slightly, then with nimble fingers traced lines.

The head fell again. The dark eyes looked at them alternately.

Clay leaned over the stone. A vertical stripe and a semicircle below, with the opening facing down.

"I do not get it.

"Nor I.

He spoke to the Indian woman again. Slowly, earnestly.

The hand picked up the brand and drew again.

"A horse or a mule," Clay said.

And the sign was repeated. This time, placed on the animal's haunch.

The two men stared at each other. For almost a minute, neither of them spoke.

"An iron" said Mac. A cattle iron.

"Yes.

"When we see one of those irons we will know ...

He shook his head.

"No, we won't know. An iron is put on all the animals of a livestock. Horses and cattle. We will only know that someone who is wearing it was the one who ...

The rain started again. The Indian woman had closed her eyes.

* * *

Two days later they began the descent. The Indian woman was sitting astride one of the mules. His face had lost the strange color.

CHAPTER II

The post.

A quadrilateral with an adobe fence and a house in the middle. Next to the house, the stables.

A pawn approached them and held their reins. A Mexican. His eyes looked at the Indian for a moment.

"Let Sally know.

A woman and two men at the door. The woman was tall, blond, in her thirties. Her hair was tied up in a thick braid. Men's shirt and trousers with white cuffs.

Clay was already by the well pump. When the water began to gush, he put his head underneath.

"Hello, Sally" said Mac.

Hello, Carrot.

A broad smile curved the woman's lips.

"Long time no see, bloody redhead.

Mac got out and spread his arms. She seemed scared.

"Hell no, you must smell like goat! Don't touch me before you take a good bath.

But she walked over to him and shook his hand.

Then he looked at Clay.

"Friend? Co-worker?

"Both" said Clay "My name is Bester.

"He likes water?

"I like.

"Come on, Carrot, you will come tired. Come in and ... what the hell are you bringing there?

"A sick Indian woman," Clay said.

"Sick? Mac, that Indian woman is a Navajo.

"It is.

"Where did you find it?

Clay had taken two steps forward.

"She is sick, ma'am. Some inconvenience? I mean, are we taking her back?

The smile disappeared from the woman's face.

"Carrot" he said, "where did you get it from?

"Listen, Sally, this is serious.

"And the girl is there in the sun," Clay said dryly. I just want to know if we have to take her.

"Carrot," she said, as if she hadn't heard him. Tell your friend that Sally Dulles doesn't leave a dog on her doorstep.

"Listen, Sally ...

"You don't need middle men, Mrs. Dulles," Clay said. We can pass the girl, right?

"Do it.

Clay scooped up the Indian woman and carried her inside. It was fresh, and it smelled good. Leather, rope and well-cooked food.

A huge fireplace in a front. A huge table and chairs. Fittings hung from nails on the walls. And the head of a cougar that gazed at them with open jaws, its fangs drawn.

"Bill, go upstairs with them and show them room seven. Let India be left there. By the way, Carrot, you damn gambusino, what disease does he have? I hope it is not contagious.

"I hope the same" said Clay, without smiling. But fortunately, I don't think so. She just has someone raped her and left her on a mountain road.

The woman turned her head slowly towards him.

"Are you speaking in...?

"I am. Completely serious, Mrs. Dulles. They did.

She took a deep breath.

"I'll go up with you, Billy" he said.

Clay dropped into a chair.

"Mac, hand me that bag of tobacco," he said.

He rolled a cigarette and lit it.

"Clay, Sally is a great woman. You shouldn't have talked to him like that.

"There are those who would not admit an Indian into their home even if they saw him dying, Mac.

"She does not.

Clay got to his feet. He climbed the worn wooden steps to the upper floor, and walked down the corridor. When he got to room seven, he entered it.

"Out! "Sally said." I will…

"Don't worry, Mrs. Dulles. I have been the one who took care of her, not the one who raped her. Now he is much better, but not quite well.

"Who was …?

"We do not know.

"Well, get out, anyway. They can eat something downstairs. I myself will say that they prepare it.

"Thanks.

He touched the Indian woman's head. She took his hand and brought it to her cheek.

"She's mute," Clay said.

Wait downstairs.

When she came downstairs, Mac and Clay were at a plate of stew, eating.

"Carrot, hell, always in trouble.

He dropped into a chair.

"Pigs" he said.

"Hell, Sally, I hope you won't say it for us.

"I say this for the men in general and in particular for those who did that.

His eyes were blue. His face, smooth; his hands strong and clean.

"Sally" said Mac. My friend is a doctor. He has cared for her.

"Shut up, would you?

Clay's voice was dry, cutting.

Sally turned to him.

"Doctor? And what does ...?

He stopped. He made a gesture with his mouth.

"Keep eating, doctor.

"My name is Clay.

"Keep eating, Clay. Likes?

"It's excellent. Yourself?

"No, my Chinese. But I taught him. Carrot, the one who did that with a girl like that is a ...

Say it.

"You can put his last name. Mac, what were you doing up there?

"What always, Sally. Looking for gold.

"Gambusino to death, huh? Why don't you feel your head for once?

"For example, I could marry you, huh, Sally?

"When you wash up every day, we'll talk about it. Now Last's stage is coming. I will have a job. We will talk later. Hey, doc ...

"Clay, Sally.

"Clay, they have the bar next door. They can have a few drinks after eating.

"Thanks. We will do it.

She stood up. In the distance came the bellowing of the stagecoach horn.

Sally went out. Clay finished and left.

Two women and two men entered. A Chinese came out of the kitchen and began to put plates on the table.

The stagecoach was in the yard, while the laborers began to loosen their harness to change their shot.

The bar was next to the house, in a shed. Mac led him to him.

"Great Sally" he said. He's been running this for five years. And, heck, he does well. Since his father died.

"I already saw it. Take a bath and ask him to marry you.

"Are you crazy? I'm not even good for licking his boots.

"No man should be fit for that, although some do.

They went into the bar. There were already five or six men in it. Behind the counter, a Mexican asked them what they were drinking.

Two of the men were evidently the postillion and the guardian. He had left his rifle on the counter.

A triangle sounded, and Sally's voice announced that food was ready. The postillion and his companion hurried out.

They drank the whiskey, slowly Clay, quickly Mac. He ordered another.

Sally came in, rolling up her shirt sleeves.

"God, how hot.

"A glass? Asked Mac.

"I can't drink with everyone. I would end up not finding the doors.

He wasn't looking at Mac, but at Clay.

"Listen, Clay. Is there no clue, nothing to make you think who could have done that?

"There is something, Sally" said Mac.

"What?

It was Clay who answered. He dipped his finger in the whiskey and moved it on the wooden counter.

"This. An iron.

The three remaining men in the bar had approached.

"An iron? A) Yes? Sally asked.

"Yes.

"How do they know?

"The Indian girl drew it like this.

"Well, I don't know any like them. And I think I know all of them.

"Everyone?

"Those of the region, yes. None of them are the same, though ...

Clay was looking her straight in the eye. The young woman frowned.

"There is one something similar, but ...

Callus. Clay waited a few moments.

"Another drink? She asked.

"You were going to say something.

"Sally, if you know any..." Mac said.

"None.

"However, Sally...

"None. Another drink?

"Thanks" said Clay.

He turned his back to the counter, looking nonchalant. The three men who had approached were parting again, each addressing his glass.

"You don't want it? Sally asked.

"Not. I do not want more.

All three men were drinking. One of them put two coins on the counter and headed for the door.

"Goodbye, Sally.

The other two followed him. Sally, Clay, and Mac were left alone.

"Sally," Mac said.

"Can't you see that he doesn't want to talk? Clay asked. Don't ask him.

"Right" Sally said suddenly. He picked up a glass, filled it with whiskey, and downed it in one gulp.

"We will take care of the girl, boys. But it certainly better get her out of here soon. This...

"Does it bother you that I'm here? "Clay said." I can pay for your stay.

"It doesn't bother me, and I don't charge when I help someone who needs it. But here it is not right. There are no conditions. On the other hand...

"What?

"Someone should give her back to her racial brothers.

"Us, for example, right?

Clay's voice was dry, cutting. Not a single word more than necessary.

"You guys brought her, guys.

"And someone... mistreated her, girl.

Sally closed her mouth. Then suddenly he addressed the redhead:

"Mac. You have been here before.

"Yes. Well, Sally, what's up with it?

"There are things that are better not to touch.

"Sally, I don't understand you... or you don't explain yourself.

"I can not talk any more.

Clay had had his back to the counter the entire time, since they were alone. Now he turned suddenly to Mac.

"Haven't you realized that if she doesn't speak it's because she's scared? And do you want me to tell you what scared her?

"Just" said the redhead. I almost think I don't need it.

"In that case, for the love of God, leave her. Let him eat his tongue. And what a good profit you do.

"You ..." Sally said.

"Yes, girl?

"You don't even know what you're talking about.

"And you know it?

"Mac can tell you that ...

"Mac will tell me what he wants, but when we're alone. And do not worry. We'll get that girl out of here and take her away. But you can be sure that if we ever bump into the son of a bitch who did the dirty job, he won't want to repeat it. Whoever it.

He spun around and faced the woman. Her face had turned red.

"I do not allow anyone to speak to me like that.

"Not? Well I'm doing it. He only has to tell us to get that dirty Indian woman out of her house, nothing more than to say it with all the words. Well then, we are going to do it.

The woman's hand shot up into the air and slapped Clay's face.

He caught her wrist and squeezed.

"Let go of me!

Clay, lips pursed, face almost white, continued to squeeze. Then, little by little, she lowered Sally's hand. She bent her knees and winced.

Clay released her.

"Don't do it again, girl.

She leaned against the counter.

"Any man would kill him for it, Clay.

"It's possible. And any woman would be ashamed not to help another who had such a thing happened to her. Let's go, Mac. This sucks.

He went to the door. Mac's face was red.

"Listen, Clay, you can't do a thing like that.

"I've done it, Mac. But if you don't like it... I'll tell you one thing: I've wanted to hit a woman for the first time in my life. And I have endured them. Is it enough for you?

He had reached the door.

"I'm going for the girl" he said. Come with me if you want, Mac. If not, I'll go off alone.

He walked to the post. When he entered the room, the table was occupied by the stagecoach travelers, they looked up at him.

He reached the ladder and began to climb it. Feeling the weight of the gazes on his back. He opened the door to room seven.

The Indian woman was sleeping peacefully, her black hair on the pillow. He stared at her, and his taut face softened. Thus, asleep, she looked like a child.

He felt footsteps and turned. Sally and Mac were arriving.

"I'm going to wait for him to wake up," Clay said. Hell, he needed it.

"Clay, you are wrong" said Mac.

"You think? About you?

"Regarding both of them, hells. Sally is not one of those. I know.

"Why don't you let her speak for herself, Mac? He has a mouth and is of legal age.

Sally closed the door behind her.

"Mac, tell him. Tell him what I told you.

"Clay" the redhead gulped ", let me tell you something.

"Well say it, with a devil.

"Clay, do you remember the three men in the bar?

"I saw them like you.

"You don't know who they were.

"No, and I don't give a ...

"Clay, wait. They are Lot Amazee's men.

Clay was looking at him.

"Speak Low. The girl needs sleep.

"You don't know who Amazee is. LA, they call it. And it does what it wants.

"What the hell does that have to do with you and me?

"He says what has to be done. And his men see to it that it is so.

"I'm still blind, Mac.

"Leave me, Mac.

Sally took two steps forward.

"Listen, man. There is no iron like the one you say the Indian drew. But there is one very similar. A cross on a circle.

Clay stared at her.

"An iron can be erased over time, or a person can misinterpret it. But it is almost certain that what the girl saw cannot be anything other than Amazee's.

Clay took a deep breath.

"Well, in that case, one of the men from that Amazee was the one who did the dirty job.

Mac looked at Sally. She gulped.

"You don't understand it yet. There are several guys on the Amazee ranch who are quite capable of doing that.

"In that case, it could have been several. There is no difference other than quantity between a herd of pigs and a single pig.

"There is. Let me speak. There are several, yes, but there is one of them, above all, that..., who would do it without hesitation. Because it is known that he has done it other times.

"Don't you get it, Clay? He is Amazee's own son, Tob Amazee.

"When women who have young daughters know that Tobias Amazee is near, they hide them in the cave" said Sally. That is if they get there in time before Tob has seen them.

Clay said:

Give me some tobacco, Mac.

Mac handed him the bag and handed him the paper. Clay rolled it up slowly.

He took the first suck.

"Like this, so easily?

Sally had her hands in her trouser pockets.

"Oh, sometimes it's not easy. The girls have parents and brothers. But then Tob also knows how to do things.

"Can't you stop his feet?

"They try. There are several crosses in a cemetery to prove it.

"Understand. And no one has tried so hard to kill him.

"It is not easy to kill Tob Amazee. No, when his father's men surround him.

"And his father doesn't stop him?

Sally smiled tightly.

"He doesn't get into it. He simply raises cattle. The rest does not interest him. There are those who say that they have once reprimanded him: «Boy, less impetus. We have all been young, but don't go overboard. " But if someone "oh, someone tried it once" wants to "really" put him around his waist, old Lot shows his teeth. «Whoever touches the puppy, take measurements first. It is not going to be that the box is small to him ». That's Lot Amazee and that's his son Tob. And that's the story.

Clay had reached the middle of his cigarette. He tossed it into a corner.

"And those guys were from Lot's ranch.

"They are. And if I had talked about the cross and the circle, in front of them ...

"What would have happened to him, Sally?

"I do not know. I don't want to think about it.

Clay looked at her. It was a vertical look, up and down, from blonde hair to boots.

"Where are you hiding when Tob Amazee arrives, Sally?

A pink color that began at the neckline that the shirt revealed, worked its way up to the woman's forehead. It seemed that the light of the sunset had entered through the window.

"Clay," Mac said.

"Don't you ever let me answer 'she'?

"Yes, Mac, you are right. Let me answer. I'm not hiding anywhere, Clay. I don't want to talk about myself anymore. No more.

The last words had been spoken through clenched teeth, coming out like a hiss.

And "he added after a moment," now you know almost everything.

"Almost, yes.

"And you know why that girl cannot continue here.

"Has Tob Amazee ever worried about the evidence of his scoundrels?

"As far as I know, yes.

"What does the sheriff say?

"Yes, to everything Lot wants. No, to what Lot does not want. That's when there's a sheriff. There is not always.

He turned to Mac.

"Carrot, tell him what happened to Lowrie Bliss. You were here. I remember. You had lost a mule and were looking for another.

"Sure, Sally. Lowrie went to find Tob at the ranch. Tob had killed a boy ...

"Busty C. He was killed in a legal duel. So legal that two of Tob's men were holding Busty while Tob put five bullets into his body. All completely "legal."

"Five bullets? Why not six o'clock, if that's what we're going to do?

"Wait a while. Lowrie went looking for him. There had been two witnesses, who told him exactly how things happened. He spoke to old Lot Amazee, and he refused to believe it. His son couldn't have done such a thing. He called him ...

He paused. His chest heaved. There was a strange look in his eyes.

Lowrie was a good sheriff. Young and strong. He knew how to handle revolvers and had been appointed by Last's board of merchants, against the mayor's advice ...

Clay narrowed his eyes.

"Did you know Lowrie?

She shut her mouth. Slowly, he brought his hand to his throat.

"I... knew him. That is enough. When Lowrie said he had proof, Lot Amazee called his son. Tob laughed. "Present them," he said.

"Who told you that, Sally?

"Enough already, Clay," Mac said quietly. Enough already. Isn't what she's saying enough for you?

"He wants to know. Why not? Lowrie was unable to present the evidence. When he was going to do it, someone killed him. A few cattle rustlers, he told himself, and they all had to believe it. But Tob... Tob... said he had been killed by a sixth bullet. He said it drunk one night at the bar.

He paused.

And then, without any intonation, as if he were reciting it:

The sixth bullet went through his heart from behind. And there Lowrie ended. There is a cross in the Last graveyard. And it's all that's left of him.

Clay took a deep breath. Then suddenly he reached out his hand.

"Sally, did I hurt you before? If so, I'm sorry.

CHAPTER III

An oil lantern illuminated the door of the post. Outside the walls, the meadow stretched to the horizon, dotted with sage.

Sally stepped out the door and looked up at the sky.

"There will be a storm soon" he said.

Mac next to her took a deep breath.

"I don't like it," he said.

"What?

"I do not know.

She gave a high-pitched hiss, bringing two fingers to her mouth. A pawn appeared at the gate of the stables.

"Yes ma'am!

"Are the last shots ready?

"Yes ma'am.

"Go to sleep.

Mac took out the bag of tobacco and began to roll the cigarette.

"You've seen?

"To the doc?

"He doesn't like to be called that. He just doesn't like it.

"How did you know him?

"In Tucson. He was drinking, I was drinking, and we ended up drinking together. When we woke up in the morning, he told me that some men knew that gold, in addition to yellow, grows in certain places. So he told me. And I understood that he had drunk too much and that he had said something.

"Something that?

"That's what I asked myself. So I told him that ...

"That you knew where there was gold.

"Hell yes. But he didn't seem interested. When we said goodbye, a guy got in between. He too had heard something. You know, Sally, a man sometimes has to let go of the brakes. You spend years looking for metal, alone, in the mountains, in the valleys, and suddenly you feel the need to talk. That guy got in the way and said we could go parties. I refused to even listen to him. And then it was armed. That man was with two friends, and all three cornered me. They wanted to make me drink to loosen my tongue. I punched one and they fell on me. And then he helped me. Details don't matter, Sally. The fact is that two of them were injured.

He paused.

"Well, Sally, and we've been together ever since.

"Is it true that he is a doctor?

"Sally, I have seen you heal that Indian girl and I asked you. He confessed it to me. But he doesn't want to be talked about.

"Why?

"I don't even know. Nor what does a doctor do looking for gold with me, here, in these places. I don't know, Sally, that's it. And he doesn't want to talk about it.

He sniffed the air and shook his head.

"I don't like it" he repeated.

"What is it you don't like, Mac?

"I don't know, Sally. But there is something I don't like. I'm an old dog in the country, and there's something about tonight that I don't like too much.

"It's getting cool" said the woman. We better go inside. Tomorrow at seven o'clock the stagecoach from Thule arrives and you have to be ready.

She reached the threshold of the door and was about to enter the house when Mac stopped her.

"Don't you notice it? "I ask.

"I don't notice anything.

"Damn, maybe I'm getting old, Sally. Well, let's go inside.

He turned around and then Sally saw.

At first he thought it was an optical illusion. It had seemed to him that something had moved in the great stage yard of the post.

He stopped, and aware that in the dark one should not stare, but to one side of the lens, he looked away. And then there was no longer the slightest doubt.

Something was moving in the courtyard. And it wasn't just one thing, but probably two.

"Mac," he said quietly.

"What's up?

"You were right. Do you have the gun there?

"By the way, Sally, but... Hell, I think...

The two figures had emerged at his side like a condensation from the shadows.

Sally felt a brutal hand cover her mouth, while another grabbed her arm, spun her around and pulled her into the house.

All this in two seconds. She heard Mac's gasp, and could still see that it was no longer two shadows, but four or five, rushing toward the man.

And then he tripped and fell to the ground. A foot came to his throat.

The door closes suddenly.

The fire in the fireplace allowed him to look, even though he had hit his back.

There were no fewer than five tall, half-naked men in the great hall of the post. They carried axes and rifles in their hands, and the flames of the fire danced on their red faces.

Indians.

Indians at the post, painted and armed Indians. Sally closed her eyes.

Mac was held by three of the Indians, while two others walked in almost complete silence toward the stairs. This seemed like a nightmare.

He heard Mac sputter something, and one of the Indians answer him.

And at that moment, the two Indians who were beginning to ascend towards the upper floor, stopped. Someone had appeared at the top of the stairs.

The hand over her mouth smelled awful and Sally gagged. Despite this, he could see that the one who had come up was Clay. And he had something in his hands.

Then they released her, and she got down on her knees. The weight he had carried on his body disappeared.

The flames caught on a half-consumed log and the scene was better illuminated.

Beside her was a dark face, and a hand that raised an ax. She realized that she should stay still and she did, but rolling her eyes toward the staircase.

"Clay," said Mac's voice.

"The first one that moves I'll kill him," Clay said. Tell him, Mac, if you can.

He had spoken in a calm but tense voice.

Sally saw the rifle in Clay's hands make a slow curve, covering a group of Indians. Mac was speaking in a broken voice, and one of the Indians was answering him.

"They don't want to kill us, Clay," Mac said, heading for the ladder.

"They just want the girl.

"So that? Tell them to release you.

The two Indians holding Mac released him, but one of them had the gambusino's revolver in his hand.

"You see it? Don't shoot, Clay.

"I'm not going to do it if they don't try to catch you again. Tell that guy to get away from Sally, to go meet up with the others.

Sally got to her feet and walked toward the stairs.

And for a moment silence reigned in the great room.

It was Mac who spoke first:

"They're from the girl's tribe, Clay. They have come here looking for it. ·

Tell them she is sick. They can't take her now.

"Give it to him," Sally intervened, still panting.

"Unless they see her.

Mac turned to one of the Indians, a tall man who appeared to be older than the others. For a moment he spoke brokenly to them. The Indian made a few sounds and then replied:

"He says he is his father. They followed our tracks here. That we have to give it back to him.

Clay made up his mind. Always with the rifle in his hand, he said:

"Tell her to come up to see her. Are they painted for war, Mac?

"No, I don't think so, at least. They are not the colors of war, as I understand it.

"Come up. And you too. No, Mac, you stay there with them, but at the slightest sign of danger, yell.

"I don't think there is, Clay.

The Indian climbed the ladder and passed Clay. He followed, leaning the rifle on his kidneys. Lastly, Sally.

The Indian woman had awakened. Seeing his compatriot his eyes widened.

The Indian approached her. Then he put his hand on her head.

He turned to Clay.

"Sick...? Medicine?

Clay nodded.

"Speak English?

"Medicine?

"Yes. Me, medicine.

The girl began to wave her hands in the air. The Indian was looking at her attentively. When he turned his face to Clay, he looked impassive. Then he said a few words.

"This should be Mac," Clay said. Those two are talking. They understand each other.

"I can see that.

The Indian woman kept waving her hands in quick gestures. He pointed at Clay and Sally.

Then at last the Indian said hough and turned to Clay.

"You... medicine?

And he pointed to the young woman. Clay nodded.

The Indian put his hand on the girl's head again and then walked to the door.

Clay and Sally followed him.

When the Indian reached the room, he addressed the others, spread his arms, and began to speak. Several times he kicked the ground with his moccasin feet. The others followed suit and growled. Mac turned to Clay.

"She is explaining to them that we picked her up after what happened to a white man.

"Who? Clay asked quickly. Let them tell you. Who?

"Does not know. He did not know him, but he saw the horse and the iron. But he has spoken some words that I do not know.

Quick, Mac, ask the old man. Tell him we want to know who did it.

"Clay, those things don't look exactly the same between them. She is the old man's daughter. You'll see...

"Don't explain to me now. Ask him who it was.

Mac spoke to the old man. He shook his head.

"He doesn't want to say it. Or do not know. There's no way, Clay.

He paused listening to the old man.

"But he says thanks to us.

The old man took two steps toward Clay and put a hand on his shoulder.

"You... medicine witch. I, friend.

"You are his friend, Clay.

"For the love of God, we are going to stop comedies. Who was the one who did it?

"You're stubborn about it," Sally said suddenly. "Mac, ask him if he was young, dark, blond... Sally, what is that guy, Amazee's son like?

"Blond.

Come on, Mac.

The Indian shook his head. Said something.

Mac nodded.

"Yellow hair" he said.

"There are more blondes on the Amazee team," said Sally.

"It's a clue anyway.

The Indian raised two fingers in the air as he spoke. "He says, Mac clarified," that they will return in two days to pick up the girl. When I'm better And they will take it away.

"Nothing more?

"Not.

The Indians had gone to the door and the old man opened it. He turned and waved his hand. Then they disappeared.

"Uff" said Sally. I've been more scared than in my entire life. And how that savage smelled.

"Mac, what the hell did you mean by saying that they saw the matter from a different point of view?

"That, Clay. For them it does not represent the same. But they want revenge because... It's something complicated.

"Be that as it may, the fact is that they are gone" said Sally. And I wouldn't want to see them reappear like they came out from under the ground.

He took out a bottle of whiskey and filled three glasses.

"I think we deserved it.

Drank. The colors returned to his face.

"They should have taken her.

"Maybe.

Clay was drinking heavily. The glass was filled again. He held it up to the light and emptied it.

"Maybe yes.

He turned to Mac.

"Mac, listen, I'm going to go talk to that guy tomorrow. Or with his father. You can come if you want.

Are you crazy? Sally asked, slamming the glass down on the table. Have you not understood what we explained before?

"Everything. I'm not stupid. But I'm also going to tell you one thing: I'm not going to leave the matter like that, understood?

"Mad. You are completely mad. And from now on I tell you that I don't want to get into that matter.

"No one has asked. Just take care of the girl. Okay, Mac!

"Clay, I'll go with you.

He frowned red.

"I don't like it, but I'm not going to leave you alone. Maybe you listen to reasons if I'm with you.

"Are you scared, Mac?

"No, Clay. I do not have it. And I already told you that we were together. I have not changed my mind. Whoever did that is a bloody scoundrel. But Amazee has a lot of power. And he will use it. You can be sure of that.

"Thanks, Mac.

"Have another drink" said Sally. And hopefully it is not one of the last to drink.

"We will try not to.

"An Indian is not a white, and Tob has done a lot... with white.

"A woman is a woman, here and elsewhere. And I don't care about the color of her hair or her skin.

"Well, the world is full of crazy.

He closed his eyes.

"I'm going to sleep, but first I'll tell the peons to bolt the doors well. Those Indians will be around.

"No, Sally. They have gone to find a man with blond hair and they know something about him.

"What, Mac?

"That he wore a sun-colored scarf around his neck. Yellow, Clay. The Indian has told him.

Clay clenched his fists.

"God, I would give anything to be able to talk to her without intermediaries. Anything, Mac. Anyone. Sally was already at the door.

"I hope no one shoots me out of the blue. I'm going to warn the peons.

"I'm going with you," Clay said.

"Well, thanks, man. I would like someone to take care of me with as much dedication as you show with that girl. Go.

CHAPTER IV

The main street of Last seemed dead in the sun. Just a few men, standing in the doorway of General Story and talking in low voices.

Clay and Mac stopped before them. The noonday sun was sinking relentlessly over the street. You could hear a guitar somewhere.

"Mac Mannister" said one of them, raising the brim of his hat. Back again, old hooligan?

"Again.

"From your clothes it would be said that you have not found gold. Not much, at least.

"Where is the sheriff? Asked Mac.

"Over there, as always. Have you looked at the police station?

"Yes. No one.

The man shrugged.

"Come in and have a drink. Who is your friend, Mac?

"A friend. We will have the drink later.

Clay had spurred his horse. Mac joined him.

"Where is the ranch, Mac?

"Five miles south. Listen, Clay, are we going to get in there, sure?

"We will go. I'm looking for a job. And you too, Mac.

"No one is going to believe it, Clay.

"It's possible. But let's look for it... there.

As they left the town, a group of horsemen advanced in the opposite direction. There were five or six of them and they rode at a long trot. They passed her without stopping.

"Did you see the one in front, Clay?

"Yes.

"Well, I'm either wrong or that's Tob Amazee.

Clay turned back.

"Already.

He didn't speak any more until they reached the turnoff in the road. A post, painted red and topped with a bucranium, from which a sign hung, marked the boundary of the ranch. The sign had a cross mounted in a circle. And under it it read Amazee Ranch.

The road wound through the meadow. Hundreds of cows and bulls moved peacefully, grazing. A little further on, a group of cowboys on horseback, cornered a point of cattle. Seeing the two companions, one of them stood out from the group and galloped over the tall grass.

Mac stopped.

The cowboy came up to them and pulled on the reins.

"Yes? "I ask.

"Yes" answered Mac. We are looking for the master.

"It's in the house. So that?

"We are looking for work.

The cowboy raised the brim of his hat and smiled.

"I think you guys are wrong. There is no work on the ranch.

"Are you the foreman? Clay asked.

"The foreman's assistant.

"In that case, if you don't mind, we'll talk to the master.

"Do it if he wants to. Everything forward.

The house was painted white and had red Spanish tiles. It consisted of several buildings and between all of them they formed a kind of square open on one side. In the middle of the space between the buildings there was another post that repeated the one they saw at the entrance to the road.

Two men on foot waited in the middle of the courtyard. Mac stopped the horse next to them.

"Good morning" he said. Master?

The man jerked his thumb toward the house.

"In there. But first they will have to tell me what they want. Its busy.

"We want work.

"There isn't. It is not time.

His tone seemed to close the discussion.

Clay leaned over his horse's neck.

"We want to speak to Mr. Amazee.

"If it was just for work, it's useless, I tell them. They can turn.

"We want" Clay's voice was insultingly patient, "to speak to Mr. Amazee.

The man looked at them, closing his eyes until they became two slits.

"Yes? Well, give it a try. Go ahead, guys.

Clay launched his horse toward the house and stopped him on the porch. A man armed with a rifle, sitting in a chair, looked at them. The point of the weapon, as if by accident, was pointed at the doctor.

"Yes?

"We want to speak to Mr. Amazee.

"He does not receive anyone. You just don't receive.

Clay blew out the air slowly.

Then suddenly he raised his voice.

"Mr. Amazee!

The man with the rifle rose to his feet.

"Where does he think he is? "I ask". In the middle of the block where did it come from? Get out of here right now!

Clay dismounted. The rifle was still pointed at him.

"Didn't you hear me?

Clay took two steps toward the porch steps.

"Now it has ...

The door opened. A tall figure appeared in the doorway.

"What a thousand the heck is going on here! Damn you sons of bitches, what's up?

The man with the rifle turned.

"These guys want to talk to you, sir.

"Those? Who are they?

The man who had just appeared had iron-gray hair, a red face, broad shoulders, and a forward belly. He gave an extraordinary impression of strength, but above all of energy.

"What do you want? Let's talk.

Clay was standing on the steps.

"Mr. Amazee?"I ask.

The question was utterly useless, but he asked it knowing that it was buying him a little time.

"Sil! But that doesn't matter to you. Who are you?

"I am looking for work.

"No work. Didn't those useless ones tell you?

"Yes, but I wanted to hear from you.

The pattern's eyes were dark gray. They were watching Clay from under thick gray eyebrows as well.

"Oh yeah? Well, turn right now where you came from and, with a thousand pairs of incarnated hells, don't bother anymore!

Clay's voice was almost insultingly calm in contrast to the thunder of that booming voice.

"Listen, Mr. Amazee, have you seen a doctor lately?

"A doctor? What the hell do you mean? Get out of here right now.

"Haven't you been feeling dizzy lately? No ringing in the ears?

"You are crazy. Buck, throw them out right now.

The man with the rifle raised this one.

"Out of here. I'm going to count to two and then ...

"Wait, damn it! What did you mean by dizziness?

"Have you felt them?

"In my life, but what did you mean?

"Nothing in that case. If it hasn't, you don't have to worry. If you have felt them, have you told a doctor?

He turned and headed toward Mac, who was still on horseback.
Come on, Mac.
He went up to his.

"Stay still there!

It had been something very close to a whiplash. Clay turned.

"Yes, Mr. Amazee?

"Come here.

"You said to get out. And they are supporting him with a rifle. We are leaving.

"You are not leaving. Buck, stop them from leaving.

"You've heard the boss, guys.

Silence fell over the patio, watered by the sun.

"Mr. Amazee, we are not willing to waste time.

"Here, the person who sent him wastes his time and whoever sent him to do it that way works. Come here.

"You heard it, boy.

Clay dismounted and made it to the porch.

"It happens in here. Buck, stay at the door and don't let that one go.

"Heard, sir.

Amazee turned and walked into the ranch. Clay turned.

"My partner comes with me.

"Your...? It's okay. Come.

Mac dismounted. He entered behind them.

There was a huge room, adorned with trophies of all kinds, from the immense head of a long-horned bull, to the skin of a bear with its huge mouth open to show its yellow teeth.

On the walls, whitewashed with lime, the torsos of antelopes, lynxes, wolves and two pumas, alternated with shotguns of all brands, calibers and ages.

"Let's see, guys, there is something here that I don't understand and I like to understand things. I can't stand it. Either I understand them or ...

He left the alternative up in the air. He went to the mahogany desk inlaid with ebony, picked up a cut crystal bottle and two glasses.

"A drink?

"Yes sir.

The old man served him and put another in front of him.

"My partner drinks too.

"Help yourself. And now you're going to tell me what the hell did you mean by that thing.

"Have you felt them, yes or no?

The old man drank before answering. He wiped his mustache.

"A couple of times. Little thing, hell. Nothing to worry about. And I did not tell anyone. How the hellish hell did you know?

Clay shot a sideways glance at Mac. Mac stepped forward. I had understood.

"My partner is a doctor, Mr. Amazee.

"Doctor? Your?

"Me.

"Why didn't you say it before? Who sent you?

"No one. Myself. I told him I was looking for a job.

"As a doctor?

"As a pawn.

"A doc? You lie. But right now you're going to tell me who told you that I ...

"Nobody, I repeat.

Clay straightened up. Then he put out his hand. The old man reached for the patterned mother-of-pearl butt of his Colt, which he wore dangling over his thick thighs.

"Hold it, damn it!

"I stared at my hand.

"That I...?

"Look at her.

Amazee obeyed.

"Do you see it steady?

"I do.

"You see her tremble. He does not see it steady. And yet, touch it and you will see that it is firm as a rock.

"Yeah, so what?

His voice was a little less confident than before.

"You are simply sick.

"Me? Don't say stupid things! In my life I have felt better!

"And those dizziness, don't you see flies before your eyes? At night he is tired. His ears are ringing.

LA found a chair and sat down.

"And all this, what does it mean? Let's assume those things happen, hell, but what do they mean?

"Have you never seen a doctor?

"Yes of course. To Dr. Ball. He comes to Last from time to time and takes out the molars and puts leeches. I made him come here and he told me it was... how was it? That it was the image of the healthy man.

Clay was staring at him. Smiled.

"Is a doctor?

"Well... he calls himself that. And now you, listen to me, doc. Is there something wrong?

"Check with Dr. Ball.

He paused.

"I have come here to look for work. Pawn. Has it?

LA rocked in her chair, back and forth.

"I have work for you.

"We are two.

"I have work for both of us. But now you're going to tell me what flashes happen to me.

Now, Mr. Amazee?

He took two steps to the table, picked up the bottle, and poured himself a new glass.

"Hire me and we'll talk.

LA stood up violently.

"Why do you want to work as a laborer? A doctor doesn't do that!

Let's say I like it better.

"Let's say that you are a liar and that you have come here for some purpose that I do not know now, but that I will find out soon.

"Let's say it and... try it. I do not care. There are other ranches where to find work.

"Quote me one.

LA's gut moved up and down. He was laughing.

"Ranches like handkerchiefs that I allow to continue still because they don't even make me the shadow that an ant would make me. Beggars who collect the crumbs of grass that I leave them. Come on, do it. Look for work in them.

"Seek health elsewhere.

LA stood up.

"What have you said?

"Go find that Ball.

He reached into his vest pocket and pulled out a piece of paper. It was folded in eight folds, and glued on a silk cloth.

"Look at this, Amazee.

"The" sir "had been put aside. The old man's eyes narrowed. But he took the paper and unfolded it.

"Doctor in medicine. I still do not understand what condemnation a doctor does here, without being there to see the sick, asking for work as a laborer.

"That's my account.

The old man narrowed his eyes. For a moment he did not speak.

"You are hired" he said suddenly.

"We are two.

"Both of us, damn it. They are hired. Buck!

Buck appeared in the doorway, rifle in hand.

"These two men are hired. Give them a place in the bedroom. They will want to eat. We do it in half an hour.

"It's okay. Report to the foreman. Buck, take them to him.

The two men headed for the door. They were already in it when the old man called him again.

"You have wanted it. He will work as a pawn.

"Naturally.

"And here people work hard. I take care of that.

"Does well. The ranch is yours.

They left. Buck was looking at them strangely.

"What the hell did you say to the boss to get him to hire you? You don't need people.

"Why don't you ask him? Clay suggested helpfully.

"I would if I was desperate for life.

They had reached one of the outbuildings. A man was examining a horse in the smithy.

"Mr. Lane, the boss has hired these two men.

Lane didn't reply. He was still examining the horse, leaning on its leg. The blacksmith was watching the scene, smoking a cigarette.

Almost five minutes passed. Finally, Lane straightened up.

"It already seems to be fine. But again don't scratch the hull.

"No sir.

And then Lane turned to them.

"So he hired you, right?

"Yes," Clay said.

Say 'yes, sir.'

"He has hired us.

Say 'yes, sir.'

Lane was tall, with very blond hair and close-set eyes, the color of dirty water. He wore a red and yellow plaid shirt and chaps on his legs.

"What's happening to you? Can't you say "yes, sir"?

"Not.

Mac already knew Clay. She saw his jaws clenched tightly, and the veins on his neck stood out against the tanned skin.

And he understood that the difficulties had begun.

"Not?

"Not.

Lane's fist shot forward, searching for Clay's jaw. He stepped back and the fist passed harmlessly past his face.

Lane's body leaned forward, arm extended.

Then Clay plunged his left fist into her right side, just above her liver.

The blow was accurate; that of a person who knows where to give, and gives hard. Lane gasped for air and fell to the ground, clutching his side with both hands.

The smith took the hammer and advanced on them.

Mac pulled out the revolver.

"Free field" he said.

"Damn," Lane said, panting.

"You started first. Not me.

Lane started to get up.

"You have a revolver on your belt. Get it out.

"Don't think about it. I have not come here to kill anyone. But you started the fight.

A group of men was approaching, almost running.

Lane put his hand on his holster.

"If you shoot a man who won't answer, you won't get out alive," Mac said lazily. Just don't think of it.

"No one is going to come hit me here" Lane said with a murderous look.

"Shut up, pig! Clay said tightly. You started. Who does he think he is? Master?

The men had arrived. They were undecided for a moment. And Lane made up his mind.

"Take those guys and put them in here. And then you close the door.

CHAPTER V

Clay realized what was about to happen. Locked up in the smithy, they would be in Lane's hands. And it wasn't very difficult to guess what he was trying to do.

"The first one who puts his hand on me, he will get a shot" he said. And he took out the gun. Mac stood next to him, shoulder to shoulder, and they faced the group.

Lane, slightly bent over, gun in hand, was staring at them. The group of men was opening up in a circle. And above, the sun was sinking incandescent over the ranch.

"Lane" said one of the men, "those two guys were at Sally's asking questions. We have seen them there.

"Oh yeah? What kind of questions?

"About a cattle iron.

Lane frowned.

"Keep them covered, guys. Let's see what condemnation that of the irons is.

But the situation was stale. The two companions covered the field as well.

"Listen, Lane, I don't want to fight. But if one of you tries to get a hand on us, there is going to be a fight.

"There will be," Lane agreed. And the only way to avoid it is for you to go into the smithy so we can talk.

"Not dead," Clay answered. And now, Lane, make way because we're leaving here.

"Yes? Well, let's see that ...

"The boss is coming" said one of the men in a low voice.

Lane turned. Lot Amazee walked towards the smithy, with heavy steps. Before reaching fifteen yards, he began to speak.

"Lane, damn it! What the hell is going on there?

Lane put the gun away.

"Nothing, Mr. Amazee. Nothing that I can't fix.

"Really? And ... may I know what you have to fix with a revolver in hand?

Suddenly his voice reached an almost thunderous degree.

"Away with all the damn weapons! Right now!

All his employees hastily put away their revolvers. Neither Clay nor Mac did. The old man's gaze turned to them.

"Have you not heard?

"Yes" said Clay "We heard it.

"Then why the hell...?

Ask Lane. He started it all.

"Lane?

The foreman moved his jaws.

"That guy was insolent with me. And I can't stand any pawn who does.

"Did you do that?

Clay smiled.

"He wanted me to give him the same treatment as you.

Lane flushed.

"You lie, you fucking bastard.

"Then we will discuss the virtues of our mothers... alone. Mr. Amazee, Lane wanted me to call you sir every time I spoke to him. Apparently he was annoyed that you hired me without him.

LA turned to her foreman.

"Lane, we'll talk later, you and me. I've hired this man and it's over. Here I give orders. And if you don't like them, you already know what you can do. And now ... with a thousand pairs of devils in bed, enough!

"One moment.

LA turned to Clay.

"Didn't you hear me?

"Yes. But the matter is not over. You have hired me, but you have not bought me. I'm free to walk away if I don't like the job... or the men. Is it well understood?

Amazee's face turned purple.

"What the hell...? Don't you know that if I wanted to, you wouldn't work in any ...?

His voice trailed off. Like a book, Clay could read her thoughts. He had asked to work as a pawn, but... he was not a pawn. And the old man had realized in the middle of his explosion.

"Out of here! "He said.

"With pleasure. Come on, Mac.

I start walking. Behind him he heard the old man's wheezing.

They reached their horses. Clay put his foot on the stirrup and then there was that rumbling again, like thunder in the mountains.

"Wait!

I hope.

The old man was approaching him.

"People are not leaving here. I miss it.

"I consider myself fired. You said "out" to me.

"And now I tell him to stay.

Clay stared at him, trying hard not to see the joy on his face at having won the round.

"With a condition.

He felt the gaze of Mac and the others on him.

"Conditions... to me?

"I am sorry. Yes.

"And ..." the voice of the old man sounded with a contained anger ", what is that condition?

"I would take orders from you, not that guy.

"I don't give a damn radish who you take your orders from...

"Not me.

"But you're going to stay. Come with me.

"Wait for me, Mac. And remember, you're with me. Don't let them put their foot down your throat while I'm with Mr. Amazee.

"Lane! Don't touch that man, do you understand me?

"Yes, Mr. Amazee.

They entered the house. The freshness of the interior welcomed them.

"I listened. "LA had turned to Clay." My ranch is run by me. If I have hired it ...

"Well, let's just drop that" Clay answered. Do you have a cigar?

Amazee went to his table, pulled out a box, and handed him a handful.

"Don't interrupt me when I speak.

"I don't want to talk about things that have already been said. You run the ranch, you give orders, and the others obey. That sounds fine to me. But nobody commands me, nor does anyone give me orders, if I don't want to.

"You asked for a job!

"I am American, white and free to hire me. And if I don't want to stay somewhere, nobody can make me do it.

"I hire him as a doctor. I'll give you a hundred dollars a month. But you have to leave me in perfect condition. I have to send 10,000 head of cattle to the North in two months.

"You have a son.

"He can't... What the hell do you mean? I am not an invalid.

"Of course. But you can become an invalid if you don't have a doctor watch over you.

"Hell, that's what I'm contracting with you!

Clay was looking at him with a concentrated expression.

"Well, what do you tell me?

"I say yes. With a condition.

"You and your damn conditions! Come on, say it now. I suppose it will be that you will only take orders from me personally.

"No sir. I will not take orders from anyone. You will receive them from me... as regards your health, of course.

LA was looking at him from under her bushy eyebrows,

"I hope nothing else. I don't think you want to run the ranch, do you?

Clay smiled.

"Not.

But his smile hadn't reached his eyes. His lips closed suddenly.

"Yes or no, Mr. Amazee?

"With a devil, we are going to try. But ... be careful. And don't excite Lane too much. He's a tough guy.

"So am I... in my own way. I've already proved it to him. Tell him to take care of the ranch and not me.

The old man suddenly laughed.

"You won't like it, but I'll tell you. And now, take away those dizziness.

"You are not going to like the way I am going to do it either.

"I listened. Almost the entire region is mine. I have earned it with my effort. But I have another part. And I have the government contracts to supply cattle to the army slaughterhouses and the civilian slaughterhouses of Chicago. I have to fulfill them. I don't want to lie in bed for two days with a headache.

"You have a son. He can handle certain jobs, right?

"He will do what he can. But I prefer to do things myself.

"Where is your son?

A look of suspicion appeared in the rancher's eyes.

"Why do you want to know? Do you want to talk to him ... about me?

"No sir.

"Because I don't want to scare the waiter. They have always seen me at my post. I don't want them to start thinking that I'm getting old.

"No sir.

"Well, in that case... let's see if we can start walking.

"Put down that glass.

"The whiskey? It's good. It's the bad whiskey that hurts me.

"Everyone hurts in the long run. Leave it.

The old man violently put the glass on the table.

"Okay, okay! It is already left. And now...

"You will now follow my instructions.

* * *

The group of horsemen entered the ranch at sunset. At the head, the young blond. Hair tousled, clothes sweaty, he entered the building, rattling his spurs and snapping his whip.

"Let's see that dinner! Hello father.

Then he found himself looking into Clay's eyes.

"Who is this? A friend?

"A doctor.

"A doctor? And why do you need a killer? Are you feeling ill, father?

"You will feel better if you follow my advice.

"Already.

He poured himself a glass of whiskey and downed it in one gulp. He clicked his tongue.

"Let's see, explain.

He was heading straight for Clay. He didn't even smile.

"There is nothing to explain. Her father and I have already spoken.

"My son Tob" Amazee said. It is a good breed puppy. Somewhat violent at times, but the grasslands don't breed peaceful men.

He put a hand on Tob's shoulder.

"Right, boy?

"Right, man. But what the heck is going on here? You've never needed a matasanos.

"Now he needs sick-curers," Clay said steely. The other noticed her tone and slowly turned to the doctor.

"Yes? What happens to him?

"Listen, Tob. Everyone reaches an age... Clay realized that the old man was quoting his own words. He did not smile. That was a good sign.

"... It is that he needs to abandon certain customs. Eat a lot. Drink a lot... Well, all that. Little by little, of course, but you have to take care of yourself.

"Silly stuff!

It had been a kind of whiplash. He turned to Clay.

"What have you done? Put fear in his body? "Not.

"Then...?

"Shut up.

"Nobody has silenced me. And if something happens to my father, say so, but no nonsense.

"Who should I tell. To you?

"Yes.

"Not.

"Father, put him in his place.

"There, son. In the place where I have wanted to have it.

"Silly stuff!

He hit his boot with the riding crop.

"Well, we'll talk tomorrow. I have ridden hard. Tomorrow.

"Where have you been?

"Well... over there. In the north of Pradera Grande. There was a carcass in the fountain. It could have poisoned the water. "He went to the door". Tomorrow we'll talk, matasanos.

Clay nodded. The boy went out. Clay walked to the window. In the twilight light, he saw someone approach him outside the porch. He recognized the broad shoulders of the foreman.

"The dinner signal is going to sound," Amazee said. You will do it with me.

Had he been scared? Clay saw the flickering light in the rancher's gaze.

"With pleasure.

The Chinese cook served dinner. When Tob saw what his father was putting on his plate, he raised an eyebrow.

"Only that? Father, a man needs food.

"Shut up, with a devil. I will eat what I want.

The boy's eyes went to Clay.

"Is that your medicine, matasanos?

"One of them.

"Father, don't let this guy tell you what to do. Come on, you've never fallen so low as to be told ...

"Shut up!

The young man's lips had narrowed into a single line.

"You and I are going to talk about all this for a bit, matasanos.

"With pleasure, Amazee. But I'm going to warn you about one thing. I don't like to be called matasanos.

"No, matasanos?

"No, and I advise you not to do it again.

"We'll see, matasanos. Although I doubt that it is even that.

Clay's eyes narrowed.

"By the way, I am. The last time I have had a chance to prove it was with an Indian girl.

"The Indians don't need doctors. They have their witches "said LA

"This one, no. Someone had raped her on a mountain road.

His eyes never left those of the young Amazee. His face looked blank, but he was staring back at her.

"Oh yeah? And what happened to her?

"It was very bad. I took care of her.

"Did you take so much trouble for an Indian woman?

"Yes.

The syllable had cracked like a lash.

"And I'd like to know who the bastard was that did it. And not by myself. The Indians are also looking for the pig that raped the girl.

"Well, let them search among them. They all know when it comes to those things.

"He was a white man, not a red man.

"How do you know?

"I know, that's it.

"So much fuss over an Indian woman? When I say that you are a matasanos ...

Clay slowly got to his feet, pushing his napkin aside.

Say that again, Amazee.

"Be quiet! "LA exploded." You, go back to your food. And you, Tob, shut up. Keep your tongue in your mouth or I'll make you swallow it.

"I'll do it myself," Clay said.

"Sit down!

Clay didn't obey. He went towards the boy and brought his face very close to the other's.

"Repeat that.

"Quack.

"Be quiet!

Clay's fist slammed into Tob Amazee's jaw and he jerked him back. The young man fell to the ground, his eyes rolling. The blow had been delivered by someone who knew anatomy well.

"Pig! How dare you hit my son?

"He insulted me.

Amazee was advancing on him.

"You don't know what you've done. I'm going to remove the skin in strips.

Clay reached for the revolver.

"Let's stop the nonsense. Nobody is going to insult me and nobody is going to strip my skin.

"Lane!

"If anyone dares to touch me, I will kill them, Amazee.

"Lane!

The foreman opened the door.

"Mister?

His eyes scanned the situation, taking over instantly.

"Lane, don't draw your revolver," Clay said quietly. Don't take it out if you're not willing to use it... to the death.

"Get off my ranch!

Mac had appeared at the door.

"Conflicts, Clay?

"Conflicts. We are left over here.

The old man's eyes were narrowed.

"Lane, I don't want to see these guys around here.

"With pleasure, sir.

"Let them go, Lane.

Tob Amazee was sitting up. His right hand went to the holster.

"Hold it, Tob!

"He has put his dirty hands on me and I'm going to...

"You will do nothing! I forbid it! These guys are leaving my ranch right now. They will not be touched by anyone.

"We're leaving" said Clay, always with the gun in his hand. We're leaving, and it would be better for them not to get ahead.

He turned to the old man.

"As for you, I have already told you: it will not take long to see the mistake you have made.

He went to the door.

"Pass, Lane.

"Lane, nobody touch him.

"No sir.

Mac and Clay went out.

"Our horses" ordered the last.

"They're going to have them in no time," Lane said ominously. And if we see them around here again, they won't have any unbroken bones.

Clay leaned into him.

And if I ever see you again somewhere alone, you will regret being born.

"Bastard.

"Not as much as you, Lane. And now, the horses. And God have mercy on you if you are not fit.

The horses were. Clay and Mac made sure of it slowly, carefully.

Then they mounted and left the ring of the ranch.

"Be very careful, boy," said Mac. Do you understand the game?

"Ample. The old man didn't want anything to happen to us inside the ranch. But outside of it it will be something else.

"Well, where are we going to go? To town?

Clay thought about it for a moment.

"Or to the post, Mac. We have to stop by Last anyway.

They arrived in town around eleven o'clock.

"We have to find a place to sleep," Clay said.

"I" Mac looked at him with a thoughtful expression, "I would find a place in the meadow. I do not like this.

"We have time for that.

They arrived at the hotel. This one had the saloon in the lower part. The place was full of people, smoke and music noise. The two companions approached the counter.

The man serving looked at them. Then, quickly, he glanced at another of those leaning against the counter. Clay was alerted.

"Mac" he said quietly. Maybe you were right. Maybe we should sleep outside.

"What's it gonna be? Asked the bartender.

"Whiskey. Do you have rooms?

"I have one. With two beds.

"We took it.

"It's three dollars.

"We take it the same.

"It's okay. Here is the key.

Clay turned slowly as Mac took the key. The man the bartender had looked at was detaching himself from the counter and walking lazily towards them.

"Look out, Mac.

The man came up to her. Then slowly he took something out of his pocket and showed it.

"I'm Hoop, Sheriff of Last" he said. And I greet the strangers when they come to town.

"Taste," Clay said.

"Yes, by the way. Nice and now give me the revolvers.

Clay leaned against the counter.

"For what reason should we do it?

"See, guys. You give them to me and then we discuss the matter, is that okay?

He was in his forties, tall, with a mustard-colored mustache. His eyes were rimmed with red.

"I asked why we should do it, Hoop.

"They do not want to?

"I have not said such a thing. I have asked the reason. There I see many men who carry their revolvers. Do you plan to ask them all?

The sheriff's gaze hardened.

"Not. To you. And I'm getting tired. Give me the artillery.

Clay spoke slowly.

"No, until I have answered.

"Not? Well, worse for you. Look up.

Clay looked up at the gallery that surrounded the saloon on three sides, there was a man with a fight. And the rifle was pointed directly at them.

"If I give the order, that man will fry them alive. So guys, go drop your guns.

"And then?

"Then they will come with me to the police station.

Clay looked up again. The rifle made a quick move.

Slowly he dropped his biricu. Mac did the same, cursing under his breath.

The sheriff kicked the guns away. Only then did the man in the gallery come down.

"Pick up those revolvers" he said while pointing their own pistols at the two companions. And you go to the door. But, boys, don't even think about running, because that would be the end.

"Come on," Clay said.

He knew when not to resist, and this was one of those moments.

CHAPTER VI

The sheriff stared at them from behind his desk. His eyes were clearly hostile. There was another commissioner next to the first.

"So you guys thought you could get to a peaceful place and start fooling around, huh?

Clay didn't reply.

"You don't answer, eh? Well, here we have ways to open the mouths of guys who are hard on it.

"What are you accusing us of, Sheriff?

"Ah, but don't you know? Very easy. I am going to tell you. To promote quarrel at Mr. Amazee's ranch.

"Did Mr. Amazee himself say it?

"That's how it is.

"Him, personally?

"That matters little, doesn't it?

"May be.

"Well, I say it doesn't matter. The fact is that you have. And we do not tolerate that here. On the other hand, guys, maybe I'm doing you a favor.

"Really?

"You can say it. Mr. Amazee's cowboys were looking for you. And without good intentions, I can assure you. So things are like this. You are going to spend a few days in the cell until things become clear.

He looked at Clay.

"They say you are a doctor.

Clay shrugged.

"It doesn't matter.

"Man no, you are not just any guy. Unfortunately, we don't need riot-promoting doctors here. Hooky, take them to the cells.

"How long are you planning to keep us here, Sheriff?

"Oh well that may be for later.

As Hooky advanced toward the inner door, the sheriff said suddenly:

"Is what I have heard about an Indian woman true?

"I don't know what you heard.

"That you found a wounded Indian woman on the mountain and took her to Sally's post.

"It is true, but she was not hurt. They had raped her.

"Well, you say that.

"Yes.

And I don't believe it. And even if it were true, an Indian is an Indian. Surely some red did. They are very fond of it.

Clay turned to him.

"That is what you would like to believe, is it not?

"That's what I think.

He put his feet on the table with satisfaction.

"Take them to the cell, boys.

Clay's jaws were clenched tight.

"Sheriff, how much does Amazee pay you to do what he tells you to do?

Sheriff Hoop's eyes gleamed.

He slowly got to his feet and advanced toward Clay. One of his commissars drove the muzzle of the rifle into the doctor's back.

Then Hoop hit Clay's jaw straight. It fell backwards.

"This is just the beginning, boy. If you say something like that again, we'll take your turn. And you will regret being born.

"Sheriff, you and I will see each other sometime when you are not protected by your thugs.

"Do you want more? Boys, get him on his feet.

Mac stepped forward.

"Why don't you fight alone, Hoop?

This time the blow was for him. The muzzles of two rifles were pointed directly at him.

"Come on, get up, kill us.

Clay stood up, and the sheriff raised his arm.

A sinewy hand grasped her wrist and pinned it into the air. Then Clay's left fist sank into Hoop's liver.

The sheriff doubled over, his mouth open, his eyes squinting. One of the marshals deflected the gun pointed at Mac and fired. The bullet passed over Clay's bent body and events began to rush.

Sheriff Hoop had fallen to the ground. He gasped for air, gasped, and a gurgling came out of his mouth.

Mac had suddenly turned on the other commissar, grabbed the rifle by the barrel and pulled it toward him. The commissioner moved. Mac raised the rifle and the crosshair hit the other, on the cheek, below one eye. He was an inch short of skipping it.

The one who had fired could not reload. Clay spun around, lifting his leg and kicking his knee into the commissioner's lower belly.

The two companions looked at each other.

"Close the door" Clay ordered.

He picked up one of the rifles and turned. The tables had turned. The sheriff was already sitting up, cursing hoarsely:

"Throw them against the wall, Mac.

Mac had seized the other weapon. With a determined look, he pointed to one of the corners. The three men obeyed.

Then Mac closed the door and barred him.

"Listen, pig.

Clay was looking directly at the sheriff.

"This is going to cost them the rope," said Hoop.

"If I kill you, it won't cost us anything, asshole. And that's what I'm going to do.

A look of alarm appeared in Hoop's eyes.

"You are not being serious.

"Not?

He raised the rifle.

"Stand up. I'm going to shoot.

The alarm had turned into plain terror.

"You can't do that, listen ...

"I'm going to shoot. I'm going to do it unless you tell me who ordered you to stop us and why.

"It was Lane," replied the sheriff, without hesitation. But he said it was by order of Mr. Amazee.

"Why?

"He said he wanted you to be in jail at least for a while.

"Why?

"No, he didn't say that.

Clay narrowed his lids.

"I think... Mac.

"Yes?

"Mac, I think I know what those damn killers wanted.

He turned violently to the sheriff and punched him in the mouth.

And you know it too.

"No, listen, I don't ...

Clay's next blow knocked out two of his teeth. His mouth filled with blood.

"And then," Clay said coldly, "I'm going to break your arms. Speaks.

Sheriff Hoop touched his mouth. His words came out almost unrecognizable through the blood.

"I think they were going to go to the post.

"Why?

"They did not say that. Word they didn't say. Only they planned to go to the post.

"Mac" Clay said in a restrained voice. Put them in the cells and cover their mouths with their handkerchiefs. Tie them up. Strong, as strong as you can. Go. As for you, if something has happened at the post, we will meet again and you can start thinking about the prayers you know ... if you know any, bastard.

Ten minutes later the three men were in the cells bound and gagged. The two companions opened the door. The street was almost empty. Only two drunks lurched across the sidewalk.

Their horses were tied at the bar. They rode. "Come on," Clay said. Run, Mac. I'm scared.

"Me too" replied the Scotsman in a low voice, "Me too.

Spurred on, the horses began to gallop.

* * *

The oil lantern gleamed over the post door. A lone figure was sprawled on the wooden steps.

They dismounted and Clay ran to the man. He was one of the Mexican peons and he was wounded or dead.

Clay jumped on his body and entered the great hall, Empty, but... in what state. The large overturned table, the chairs on the floor and a cauldron with food scattered at the entrance to the kitchen.

"Sally!

Clay had screamed as he ran for the stairs.

"Don't move," said a voice. Don't move or by God I killed him.

"Sally!

Clay had stopped at the first landing. At the top of the stairs, a rifle moved in the indecisive light of a lantern hanging from the wall.

Mac had entered in turn. He stopped in the middle of the room.

"You...

The woman descended a step. The rifle shook slightly in his hands.

"Sally, what happened?

The woman stepped into the cone of light from the lantern. His blond hair hung down covering part of his face. But he did not hide the slight stream of blood that stained his forehead and part of his cheek.

"You ..." he repeated.

Clay took the steps two at a time, followed by Mac. He picked up the rifle and took it from her hands.

Sally sank down on one of the steps and cupped her face in her hands.

"I thought... it was them again.

"Are you hurt?

"Me? I think it is...

He touched his forehead with his hand and looked at it.

"It's nothing... I think.

Clay took down the lantern and held it close to the woman's face. He closed his eyes.

Clay quickly examined the wound. Just a cut.

"Is there something more than this?

"I... no, I don't think so, although... they beat me.

He opened his eyes.

"The damn bastards beat me.

"Sally, stand up.

"Why...?

"I want to know if they have done anything else to him.

"No, just hit me. They hit me with a strap on my back.

Clay turned it over. Her dress was torn. You could see the reddish stripes of the blows, crisscrossing.

"Someone's going to pay for this," Mac said thoughtfully.

"And ... they took the Indian," she said in the same colorless voice.

"Where?

"I do not know. They didn't tell me. Only they took her.

He leaned against the railing.

"Is anyone going to pay, Mac? Who will make you pay for it?

"Sally, listen ...

"Who, damn? Who is going to make you pay for it?

His voice had risen to a squeak. Clay slapped her twice. She opened her eyes wide and then suddenly she started crying.

"Mac, make your bed. I'm going to take her.

He took her in his arms and, guided by Mac, they reached the bedroom. He left her on the bed.

"Sally, can you hear me?

"Yes of course. I am sorry. He had to scream.

"I know. Do not worry. But I don't want hysteria now. Sally, who did it?

"Lane. The foreman of ...

"I know him," Clay cut in dryly. I know who that damn pig is.

"It was him and four of his men.

He was staring at Clay.

"Sorry, Clay. They came suddenly and beat my boys. Then they entered the post and frightened the horses. I don't even know if I can get them together again.

He pursed his lips. Clay was cleaning the wound on his forehead.

"Lane told me this would happen to everyone who helps the bloody Indians. It was his words. And that they were going to teach her a lesson. When I tried to stop them, they beat me.

"Who? Lane?

"Yes. He had me hold by two of them and then hit me with his belt.

"Sally, was Amazee's son among them?

"I didn't see it, Clay. I did not see it.

"The wound is nothing. I'm going to look in the Indian room. Mac, give Sally some alcohol.

He came back after a moment. His face was deathly pale.

"They must have hurt her. There is blood on the bedclothes.

Suddenly Mac seemed to go crazy. He picked up his hat and tossed it to the ground. Some remote Celtic ancestor seemed to come out of him. Clay had never seen him like this in their time together.

"I will kill them, by God in heaven! I swear I'm going to kill all the fucking sons of bitches and may God condemn them in hell!

"Mac.

"I swear!

Clay took him by the arm. He squeezed hard.

"Mac, enough already. I think the same that you. But stop it, damn it! This is not the time to swear, but to act. Shut up now!

He turned to Sally.

"Where could they have led India?

Sally shrugged.

"I do not know.

Mac was still shaking. He opened his eyes.

"Someone may know.

"Who?

"The Indians.

"We'd have to find them first, Mac. It's no use to us. But if we don't know where they took her, at least we know where we can find Lane. Sally, get ready. Let's go.

"I can't move from the post. In the morning the mail will arrive to change shot. I can not.

Clay thought about it for a moment.

"Just like that we can't move in the middle of the night. Let's see what happened to the pawns.

They went down. The man at the door had regained consciousness.

"When was all that? Clay asked. When it happened?

"About half an hour ago, Clay. Maybe a little more.

"They have been able to run a lot in that time. How are you?

The man sat up. He had a head injury.

"I do not know. It hurts.

"Enters.

They reached the shed where the peons slept. There were only two, tied to the bunk beds and with signs of having been beaten as well.

When he had everyone in the living room, while Mac gave them coffee and whiskey, Clay asked:

"Do any of you know how to follow tracks?

One of them nodded as he drank.

"Me, sir.

"Tomorrow we may have to use you.

The man denied.

"I'm sorry, ma'am, but... we are leaving.

"You can't do it" Sally replied with tight lips. You can't leave me like this now.

"They told us that the next time they came back they would kill us, ma'am. We are not staying. No one will bother them if they kill people like us.

"They're right," Clay said. There is no law that protects them.

"By now they will have unleashed the sheriff," said Mac. Sally looked at him in amazement.

Clay explained it to him in a few words.

"But... in that case at this time you are outside the law.

But was it even here?

He hit the table hard.

"Sally, we are not going to argue any more. When the mail comes, let him handle it however he can.

"I can not do this.

"We will see it in the morning. Meanwhile, we are going to rest. Mac, shut the door tight. Catch it. We will rest until the light comes. We simply cannot do otherwise.

He took Sally by the arm.

"Come on, don't worry. Come on.

"Don't worry me ...?

"Now, no" he repeated firmly. Let's go to his room.

He led her to him. At the door he took her by the shoulders.

"I'm sorry about all this. It was our fault, but we didn't know what to do with that poor creature.

"I told them to take her away... Oh, I'm not thinking about what those beasts have done here. I am thinking about her.

"I know. But I'll tell you one thing, Sally: this is not over. Mac said it screaming and I said it softly. They will remember it for the rest of their lives.

She took a deep breath. Beneath her torn dress, her breast rose perceptibly. There are times when the weight of external circumstances works on you and acts for you. Clay leaned over her, wrapped his arms around her, and pressed his lips to hers. She didn't even try to resist. He responded to the hug and the kiss.

When they parted they looked straight into each other's eyes.

Go to sleep, Sally.

* * *

The sun rose red on the horizon. Very red, almost bloody.

Mac looked at him with the eyes of the man who has lived all his life in the country.

"There will be a storm soon" he said. Before noon.

By his side. Clay, half naked, washed in the trough.

The three peons poked their heads out.

"We're leaving" they said.

"Go.

"U.S...

"Go away.

They walked away.

"Look" said Mac.

There was a group of horses on the other side of the fence. Sally appeared at that moment at the door.

"The food... Oh!

He had seen the horses.

"Let's get them. They will not be very rested when the mail arrives, but... it is the only thing there will be.

"Come on, Sally, we'll help you.

They collected the horses and placed them in the stalls. Mac cleaned them up quickly. It was at the moment he was leaving that they saw the head on the fence.

"They're there," Sally said tightly in a low voice. Look at them, they are there.

They were now two heads. Each of them wore a turkey feather amid her black braided hair.

"Mac, tell them to come in.

Mac raised his voice and said something. The two Indians jumped over the fence and approached them.

Their bodies were full of dust. The dark painted faces. The bleary eyes.

"Mac, tell them what happened.

Mac spoke for a few seconds. The two Indians looked at each other. Then one of them took out his tomahawk and held it up in the air while chanting something.

"What does it say?

"I do not know. It seems like a spell, but I don't understand it. Perhaps...

He spoke to the Indian. He didn't seem to hear him, but when Mac finished, he replied:

"He says they will follow those men and kill them.

"No, tell him no. Just tell them to tell us where they can be. Have them look for their prints and let us know if they find anything.

"Clay, you don't understand. They have to get revenge. It is their law, as we have ours.

"Talk to them at least.

"They have to get revenge, Clay.

"Okay, but tell them to look for the prints.

Mac spoke to them. One of the Indians disappeared towards the door and began to search the ground. Then he squawked something.

"They found them, Clay. I think they found them.

Clay and Sally headed toward them. One of the Indians was pointing to the horizon with his finger. Towards the mountains.

"I understand" said Clay Bester through clenched teeth. Understand. They want to get rid of the evidence. God, someone is going to pay for this with blood and flesh.

"What are you going to do? Sally asked.

Clay looked at her.

"You can't stay here, Sally, at least not alone. And I want to follow those individuals. Take Mac to town.

"Wait a bit, Clay," Mac said. Sally won't be safer in the city than here. Remember the sheriff. It's sold to LA. They'll find a way to... push her. You may even be in danger.

"Wait 'both of you'" Sally said, her face flushed with anger. You are talking as if I am not in front of you or tell what I want. I have run the post since my father died and I am not going to leave it. It feeds me and I like it.

Clay looked at her.

"Listens. If the post is not attended because you have been attacked, someone will have to do something, right? Things will get tangled, there will be protests, there will be trouble on the line.

Mac opened his mouth.

"Hell, it's an idea.

"But ..." Sally was thoughtful for a moment. " Yes, the Overseas will have to do something. The inspectors come here every month and some twice a month. Yes it's correct.

"You have run out of pawns. You cannot do otherwise. Let the Overseas claim LA for a part. And we are going to claim him for the other.

He stretched out as he looked at the Indians, who were conferring as a group.

"Mac, ask them what they are going to do.

Mac obeyed. He turned to Clay.

"They say they will follow them until they find them.

"Mac, I'm going to go with them. You stay with Sally and if someone comes... get them shot. You have understood?

"But you don't get along with the red ones ...

"No matter. Do what I say. Tell them I'm going with them.

CHAPTER VII

All morning Sally and Mac were very busy trying to calm the mail travelers. He was finally able to get out, but Sally told the postillion to warn the Overseas inspector in Tucson that there were no laborers because the post had been robbed and the employees had been fired.

Then they waited. Mac, rifle in hand, had crouched on the roof of the house.

At three in the afternoon they saw the solitary figure approaching the horse's stride.

"Sally" said Mac. It's Clay.

The girl opened the door and crossed the courtyard. At the entrance he waited.

Clay came up to her. His head was lowered to his chest. Only when he was next to the girl did he raise his eyes.

"And ..." Sally said.

"Dead" was the reply.

Sally raised her hand slowly to her face.

"Dead? Have you ...?

"One shot.

"Happens. You will be hungry.

"Not.

"But you have to eat. Come on, I've prepared something for you.

Clay dismounted and slapped the horse on the rump.

Mac had descended. A single glance at Clay's face made him close his mouth, which he had already opened to ask:

Clay sat down at the table. Sally set a plate before him.

"I do not have...

"Eat.

Clay began to eat in silence. The other two were waiting.

"Damn," said the doctor suddenly. Curse.

"Scream," Mac advised him.

"It is not necessary, Mac. I am holding back and I can do it.

He raised his eyes.

"They have shot her in the chest and left her on a stone, Thus, so simply a young life is extinguished.

He reached into his vest pocket and pulled something out, which he kept hidden in his fist.

Sally had her head lowered. Mac was muttering under his breath as if praying or cursing.

Clay got to his feet.

Then he opened his hand and put something on the table.

It was a piece of lead flattened at the tip. A bullet.

"She is the one who killed her" he said. And with her ... Sally, do you have anything to drink?

"Yes.

It served.

And the Indians? Asked Mac.

"They have taken the body. I don't know what they are going to do. I wish you were there, Mac, but you don't really have to. Now I know what I'm going to do. Can I lie down for a while?

"Come.

Sally led him into one of the rooms. Clay threw himself on the bed without even removing his boots.

"Tell Mac if someone comes to wake me up. I want to sleep until the night.

Sally stared at him. Then, seeing him close his eyes, she went to the door. Once in it he turned again.

* * *

Clay came downstairs when it was already dark. He went out to the patio and rolled a cigarette. A shadow appeared beside him.

"What are you going to do, Clay?

"Find the man who did it. There is something the old Indian said, the girl's father. You remember?

"Not. I think not...

"A handkerchief, Sally. A yellow scarf. Someone has one and that someone is the one who did it.

"Understand. And later...

"I do not know.

He put an arm around the woman's shoulders.

"Sally, I'm sorry for everything that happened to you because of us.

"Oh, drop it.

They were very close. The strong scent of blooming sage rose from the meadow.

She raised her face. Clay leaned down and kissed her.

* * *

The dawn light was already streaming through the window. Outside they heard Mac's heavy footsteps.

"What are you doing here? She asked in a low voice. Why is a man like you here, chasing a phantom gold in the company of that old hooligan? Or... maybe I shouldn't ask... anything?

"Now yes. You can ask. I came from the East trying to forget something that happened there.

"Something or someone?

"Someone.

"A woman?

She looked. Then a slow smile appeared on his lips.

"No, a child. My brother. He got sick and I wanted to take care of him. I didn't want him to go to the hospital. Some colleagues told me that I could not save it by myself. I tried and ... it died.

"I am sorry.

"They told me I was not to blame, but... the next time a child was brought to my office, I understood that there was nothing I could do for him. I just couldn't. It was beyond my strength. Every time I looked at him, my brother's face would come between him and me.

He paused.

"And that's it.

She breathed heavily.

"I am sorry. But have you decided to leave your profession?

"I had decided until I saw that poor girl. Then I don't know. I don't know, you understand?

"Yes" she whispered. And now I think we should get up. Mac must wonder where we are.

"Ask him... if he does.

Mac was waiting for them by the door. The eggs and ham had already been fried and the smell permeated the room.

He didn't even look at them. He just set the dishes before them. Clay smiled.

"Good," said Mac, as he sat down. What are you thinking to do?

"First of all, are you still with me?

Mac attacked his food.

"I don't say things more than once. I told you before. But I will make you a clarification: gold exists. It is waiting for us. This time I'm not mistaken, Sally, don't look at me like that.

"It can wait," Clay said.

"As you like. We are partners. I just wanted to make that clear to you. And now ... you speak.

"Listen, both of you. I'm going to look for the blond man who wears a yellow scarf around his neck. You and me, Mac, we know where it is. At the ranch in LA So we're going to look for him there. And when I find him I'm going to call him the son of a very big bitch and I'm going to kill him.

"Forgives. You are not going to kill him before I speak to him a few words.

"It doesn't matter. Sooner or later ... I'm going to kill him.

"A doctor saves lives, he does not kill them" Sally said suddenly.

"Well in front of you you have one that is going to end at least one life.

The answer had been given in a brutal tone. Sally opened her mouth and closed it again.

"A chatting life doesn't end," Mac said scolding.

"I know. And so...

Outside there was a braying.

"It's one of our donkeys," Mac said, standing up. Someone is coming.

He went to the door and opened it, but not quite peeking out.

"Yes" he said. Someone is coming. Clay, come on.

Clay walked over to him.

Very close to the fence of the post there was a group of men.

Clay's face was deadly serious when he pulled out the revolver.

"Wait," Mac said slowly. I'm going upstairs with the rifle. And you'd better close the door and wait inside. Believe it or not, there are Tob Amazee and several of his men.

He picked up the rifle and went to the stairs.

The men had reached the patio door, the stage entrance.

Ahead was a man in a fancy vest riding a long-maned white horse.

"Sally! He yelled, as he tugged on the reins.

"Don't answer," Clay ordered.

Sally didn't reply. He had walked to the wall and taken down one of the rifles.

"Sally, we know you are there! Salt!

The young woman handed Clay the rifle. Then he picked up another for her.

"Won't you go out? Well, we will go in. I want to talk to you.

Clay checked that the rifle was loaded. It was a "Winchester" and looked in very good condition. He waited almost a minute still. Mac must have made it to the roof by now and out the hatch.

Then he opened the door and stood in the doorway, legs spread wide, rifle in hand. The arm, bent.

"Yes? "I ask.

Tob Amazee put his hand to his head and raised his flat top hat slightly.

"You, matasanos?

Clay didn't reply. The tip of the rifle was raised slightly.

What the hell are you doing here?

Clay didn't reply. I expected.

"Don't you want to answer? Well, I'm going in.

Clay didn't reply.

"Come on, answer! I'm going in.

"Come in, Tob" Sally said behind Clay. What are you waiting for?

"Wait a minute" said Clay. Is Lane with you, Amazee?

"No, kill us.

"Well then, come in, pig.

There was a silence.

"What did you say? Tob asked in a white voice.

"I said come in, pig. You think I'm a crook. I think that you are a pig and a ruffian, and some other things that I keep quiet because there is a lady in front of you. Now come on in, little man. I hit it once. Apparently he has not had enough and comes back for more. To your taste. I have met some men who like to be beaten. Come on in, pig, little one.

One of the men spoke.

"Ignore it, Tob. It is challenging you. There is a man on the roof and he has a rifle.

Tob raised his head.

"What did you expect? Clay asked. Finding a lonely woman and scared pawns again? Come on, come in at once, asshole!

"You," Tob said slowly, "you're dead already, man."

"A dead man wouldn't have it nailed there, stupid. And now, either they enter or they go the way they came. But if you want to see Sally again after you've hit her with a leash, come in.

"I haven't hit Sally.

"His men... well, those pigs did. It does not matter.

Then suddenly he yelled:

"Come on, come in at once, you filthy coward, you bastard! His old man would have already done it.

"I'm going in. And you are not going to ...

"Don't threaten, pig! Take action! Between.

One of the men behind Tob lowered his hand to his leg. The rifle was raised again.

"You have wanted it.

And shot. The bullet passed between the horse's ears and struck the man in the chest.

He fell to the ground, perching. Mac's voice was perfectly heard from above.

"I've got them covered, Clay.

Clay smiled. Smoke billowed into the still air.

"Tob, are you going in or not? But if he doesn't come in now, I'll say everywhere he's man enough to hit a woman, but not enough to stand up to someone wearing pants.

Tob slowly dismounted. His face was pale.

"Tell your men to stay still, Tob. You are covered by two rifles.

"That's what it's worth.

"Wait and you will find out soon, Tob. We are waiting for it.

Tob couldn't do otherwise. He walked toward the house, crossing the large courtyard.

Clay stepped aside, a crooked smile on his lips.

"Inside, Tob, lonely cock. Let `s go inside.

Tob passed her. Livid, with clenched teeth.

"Mac! If any of them make the slightest move, shoot. Kill the damn yellow dogs!

"You" said Tob.

"Come on, stop the nonsense. Pass at once.

Some voices were heard outside.

"They won't do you any good, Tob. They are well covered. And now...

Sally was standing by the table. He also had the rifle in his hand.

"Is it true that you have been beaten, Sally? Asked the boy.

"Do you want to see the signs?

"I did not do it.

"Your little friend Lane did it.

"The same," Clay said slowly, "who killed the Indian girl. Or at least someone did it on his orders, Tob. Always following your orders.

Tob turned to him.

"What does he say about India?

"Ah, but don't you know? Take off your revolver, Amazee. Drop it to the ground.

"Nobody orders me, kills ...

Clay raised the rifle and shoved it to his throat. He pushed hard and the boy's head jerked back. He backed away and tripped over a chair.

"Shut up, pig," Clay said in a low, strained voice. Shut up and don't repeat that word again. You've already worn it.

He put down the rifle and hit the other in the face over the mouth.

Tob grunted and reached for the revolver.

Sally couldn't remember seeing anything like it. It was as if a typhoon had suddenly crashed down on the boy.

Clay hit him in the stomach, face, and ears. A complete series that toppled the other like a log in the middle of the room.

Then Clay leaned over him, disarmed him, and pulled him to his feet, holding him by the collar of his shirt.

"I have a bullet in store for you" he said, putting his face very close to hers. The same bullet that killed the Indian girl. I keep it to stick it in the heart of the bastard who did it. And now...

A shot snapped overhead.

"Other! Howled Mac. Come on, you disgusting, move again!

Tob opened his eyes.

"I have not killed any Indian.

"You raped her.

"I didnot do that.

"So Who?

"I do not know. And if you take your revolver ...

"And you yours? Amazee, don't make me laugh. Why do I want a revolver when I have it on my knees? And now, bastard, who did that to the Indian woman?

"I do not know.

"Wasn't it you? Or are you afraid to say it? There are things that are done, but that are not discussed, except in a bar and among friends, right?

"I did not make it.

Clay clenched his mouth.

"Sally, are you strong?

"I am, Clay.

"I'm going to put some pressure on this brave rooster. I am going to spread it on that table and use with it some of the instruments that we matasanos use. Have you heard of scalpels, ruffian?

It hit him in the mouth.

"Answer when I speak to you. Haven't heard of them? They are knives as sharp as those used by the Indians to scalpel. More much more. They serve to operate. With one of them, I can cut the skin off your back until the flesh is exposed. And all this without killing you. You fancy?

"The sixth bullet" Sally said suddenly ". The sixth bullet that killed Lowrie Bliss. Do you remember her, Tob?

A new expression appeared in the boy's eyes. Clay couldn't be wrong about its meaning. It was fear, real fear.

"Sally, I didn't kill Lowrie ...

Clay's fist slammed into his chin.

Tob fell to the ground, his eyes rolling. Rifle in hand, Clay leaned out the door.

"You guys.

There were three men left. The three of them, standing still, on their horses, at the door of the patio.

"And take off your hats.

All three men roared at the same time. A cowboy can go completely naked, but he will keep his boots and hat.

"And drop your weapons on the ground! Come on Mac, if they don't, start shooting!

Slowly, growling curses and curses, the three men began to obey. A moment later the weapons were on the ground.

"Kick them away!

They did it. They knew when they shouldn't disobey. There was a rifle pointed at them and their boss was inside the house and in Clay's possession. They had no choice but to do so.

Clay went out, collected the weapons, and carried them back into the house. The boy was beginning to regain consciousness.

CHAPTER VIII

Clay grabbed him by the lapels, lifted him to his feet, and led him to the table. Sally, with a quick movement, swept away all the things that were on her.

Tob looked at the two of them alternately. What he saw in the eyes of the others galvanized him.

"You cannot crucify me. They can not!

"Not? You're going to see it, you dirty ruffian. Now you don't have daddy to defend you, huh? Have you lost your guts?

"I have not lost them. But I have not done what you say I have done.

He was trying to speak calmly, but fear was evident in his eyes. He swallowed frequently and his complexion was yellowish.

"Someone has made them for you, or carrying out your orders. Where is Lane?

"I do not know. Word I don't know. He has acted on his own.

"You killed Lowrie from behind," Sally said.

"Not true, Lowrie turned his back on me...

"You lie, pig. Go ahead, Clay, why don't you ...?

"Answer once and for all, pig. But I don't want any more evasions. Answer back. Was it you who did that with the Indian woman?

"Not.

The answer had spilled out of her mouth quickly, but she had taken her eyes off Clay's when she answered, and Bester noted it.

"You went.

"Not. It was Lane.

And you knew it. Were you there

"Not. Lane told me later. Word that was him.

"At least" said Clay, I know he was the one who took her from here and who killed her. Where is your yellow scarf?

"I don't have any... Hey, doc, Lane has one. Word. Has it. I have seen it many times.

"So it was Lane.

"I... told him that he had done wrong.

Clay hit him again with a disgusted face.

"And above, coward. And this was the superman that everyone told me about? Come on, Sally, there you are, shaking and accusing your partner of wrongdoing.

"I see it and I feel like giving back.

"What are you going to do with me? Tob asked.

Clay turned to him.

"You will see it right away.

He removed her belt and tied her hands with it behind her back. He squeezed well, wanting to hurt.

Then he took it out into the yard.

"Men!

The three waited, heads in the air in the middle of the courtyard.

"Tob, are you okay? Asked one of them.

"At least he's alive," Clay replied.

"When Mr. Amazee sees what he has done with his son, you will not know where to go" replied the same man.

"Wait until you know what I'm going to do.

"You won't think of killing me, doc.

"I am going to put a gun in his hand and take another one. And may the one who kills the other sooner win.

Tob's eyes let a small bluish flame pass. Hope returned to him.

"You think you are very good with weapons, right?

Tob didn't reply. He didn't want to lose the advantage he imagined he was getting. He didn't want to irritate that demon.

"But before...

He turned to the three remaining men.

"One of you is going to look for Mr. Amazee and tell him that I have his puppy in my possession. And if you want it back, you will have to hand me over to Lane.

Tob swallowed again.

"Hey, listen, I think we can fix this better...

Nonchalantly, Clay hit him on the mouth. Blood spurted from the young man's lips again.

"Speak when I allow it, chick. Come on, draw lots among you who is going to go with that embassy to old LA. And I hope they don't do like the eastern kings: they killed the bearers of bad news.

He turned back to the house.

"Mac, come down. You have to do something down here.

When the other got to the patio:

"Tie up those guys and put them inside the house. Tie them all together. And good.

"Don't worry, boy, I know how to tie a few knots that won't untie.

"Well... let's do it!

He put his arm around Sally's shoulder. She raised her head to him.

"You are ... a demon" he said with some fear. A true demon.

"Do not worry about it. I am not always.

The men were tied up in a group after a moment. Only one of them was free of ligatures. Clay faced him.

"And now, go to your master and tell him what has happened. That here is your son. And if he pretends ... take a good look at what I'm saying: if he wants something against us, his son will die.

"Yes" said the man swallowing hard.

"Well... run, damn it! Run and don't stop.

The man obeyed.

The Overseas inspector arrived at two in the afternoon mounted on a horse. Sally was waiting for him at the post door.

"Sally, what the hell...?

Come in, Hough. I'm going to tell you.

The inspector was a gray-haired man but not old.

He looked at the prisoners tied up in the corner. He raised an eyebrow.

"Sally, those...? Isn't one of them the son of old Amazee?

"The same. Sit down. I'll fix you something to eat.

"Yourself? And the Chinese?

"He left the same as the others. They were beaten and I myself... look.

She pulled her blouse off her left shoulder. Hugh stared at the welts.

"That was? He pointed to Tob.

"Your overseer, Lane's filthy beast.

"I think I know him. Okay, Sally, something has to be done.

Clay and Mac had just appeared on the stairs.

"Hough, this is the men who helped me. And now let me explain.

Hough shook hands with both men. Then he sat down. Sally put the food on a plate and as she ate it, explained everything.

When he finished, the inspector nodded.

"I understand that you couldn't do anything else, Sally, but perhaps you shouldn't have admitted the Indian woman to the post.

"Is that what you think, mister? Clay said through clenched teeth.

The inspector raised a hand in the air.

"Wait a minute, doctor. I am speaking from the point of view of the Overseas. That is what they will say. Please understand that it is not my personal opinion.

"So I understand it.

"Well, now we have to see what we do with the post. The next trip is at six in the afternoon, right? You have horses?

"I got them. Those of those guys who are there, in addition to the ones I have left.

"The Overseas could be accused of robbery of shots.

"If you say in your report what happened, the Overseas people will be very stupid if they don't understand.

"I said they could be charged, not that they don't understand. Well, whether they do it or not, I am in charge of saying what to do in an emergency. And we are going to use those horses, because this is an emergency.

He leaned back in his chair and lit a cigarette.

"I will understand myself with the mandarins of the Overseas. And I'm going to file your complaint, Sally. Against a certain Lane, right?

"That's right, Hough. And three more men.

"Agree. Do you know their names?

"One of them is called Tom, and another is called Spider. The third I knew only by sight. I do not know their names.

"Already.

He took the girl's hand.

"Sorry, girl. But do not worry. The Overseas has long hands. And a lot of strength. Even if your life becomes impossible here, we will find some other place for you. You are a good post manager, and we are not so overloaded with honest managers.

"Thanks, Hugh, but I'd like to stay here.

"We can talk about that later" Clay said suddenly. They turned to him.

"Yes doctor?

"We'll talk later.

"And in the meantime, the next trip will come. We will attend to you in the absence of anything else. I've already said in Tucson to send in new pawns. But this time they will be armed men, vigilantes of the company, who will not be intimidated by these guys. Tomorrow I'll go talk to old Amazee.

"So that? Clay asked.

"How? Excuse me, doctor, I don't understand. I have to talk to him about what happened here.

"For this you will not need to go to the ranch. Amazee will come here when she finds out we have her little boy taken.

"I cannot be still while it comes or it does not come.

"It will come, don't worry. You can't leave your son here. Because...

He paused.

"He knows that I am willing to kill him if he does not come.

"Understand. But I can't do things like that. The Overseas inspectors have, in a way, an official position. We can even act as sworn bailiffs.

"That's your thing, Hough. Instead I know what I want to do.

"I wouldn't advise it, doctor.

"Don't advise me then.

For a moment, the atmosphere became tense.

It was Sally who poured oil into the waves.

"We can wait a bit until the trip comes, right? Later we will talk about all that.

"Agreed for me" said the inspector. The sending men will arrive here tomorrow morning. Meanwhile, we are going to prepare the reception for the next trip.

The relief was hardly any incident. The guide protested a bit about being given non-draft horses, but when Hough explained what had happened, he fell silent.

Then they were alone again. Hough lit a cigarette.

"Listen, doctor. I'm sorry about this I'm going to tell you, but I have no choice but to do so. The men who come on the way do it to defend the interests of the Overseas exclusively.

Clay looked at him seriously.

"I haven't asked for your help, Hough. I think I've shown that so far at least I know how to deal with myself... well, with Mac.

"I know and that is not what I mean. I mean actually, I personally think you did well, and Sally did the same. But I could never convince the mandarins of the Overseas that their men should defend our views. So if the post is attacked, or Sally, those men will take up arms.

"No one has asked you for anything else, Hough," Clay repeated with the same intonation. And if you think we are in the way of the post or may cause incidents with our presence there, we will leave right now. All I wanted by staying was to prevent something from happening to Sally.

"I told you that I understand, right?

Then he went outside to smoke. Sally turned to Clay.

"You shouldn't have told him that. He is one of the best and straightest men there is.

"I don't give a damn about that now. I plan to leave.

"And... where will you go? Looking for the gold?

"No, until I have finished what brought me here. No, until I'm done with that damn Amazee and his henchmen. No, until ...

Then he took her in his arms and squeezed her.

"Do you understand?

"Y...? "she said". When you're done, you'll go, right?

"Yes.

"I guess... you don't care about me.

Clay didn't reply. He just looked at her.

"Yes or no?

"You know it. Yes.

"But you will go away.

"Yes.

"Understand. Everything has been ... a chapter. I think it goes like this.

Clay lit a cigarette.

Come with me, Sally.

"Me...?

She put her hand to her chest and then dropped it. His face was pale.

"You mean I go with you like ...?

Like my wife.

She forced a smile.

"Gentleman, so much honor ...

"Shut up. Don't go down that road.

"How do you want me to respond? Falling into your arms?

"You already fell" was the reply. She closed her eyes.

"Clay" he finally said. There are other ways to ask a woman ...

"I have no time. Come with me.

"Let's see if we can speak sensibly. Why do not you stay?

"In the lands that old chief dominates? Never.

"Clay, I ...

"Don't answer me now, will you? Do it when everything is over.

"What if you are the one who ends?

Clay shrugged. There was no answer. She crossed and uncrossed her arms over her chest.

"Okay, ask me then.

"I will do it. Between that Indian woman and you have... we could say that you have awakened the desire to live in me again. To live and work.

"What about the gold, Clay?

"Oh, the gold. I'll help that good old Mac find it and take it away. He has earned it after so many years of fighting life for him. I don't want it and I hope you don't either.

"For me... Ask me later, Clay. Or ... drop the matter and let's go. You see "he smiled softly." I am answering you now.

"I will not abandon it. Would you think the same of me if I did?

"I do not know i do not know. Don't ask me. I want you to do what you want to do, not what I want.

"Then...

Hough found them hugging. He coughed discreetly.

"I think" he said, that events are approaching.

CHAPTER IX

It seemed like the scene was repeating itself over and over again. When Clay peered out the door, he saw a group of horsemen advancing toward the post. They stopped at the door to the stagecoach yard.

Clay quickly counted them. There were no less than fifteen.

"Mac.

"Yes, Clay. I'm going to the roof.

"Hough?

"Don't worry, doctor. I'm here.

"They are coming for us.

"Let me speak. I am in what we could call my properties.

"For the moment, I'm in control, Hough. Are you going to attack me from behind?

"No, of course not. I just want to warn you that ...

"Yeah, the Overseas and all that. I already know it. At the moment I am the one issuing the orders here.

Hough was silent. Whether or not he agreed, that didn't matter much to Clay now.

Then a man broke away from the group and advanced into the great courtyard.

Clay quickly gauged the situation. All the newcomers were armed with rifles and carried them not in their bunkers, but in their hands.

He recognized perfectly the tall stature and bulk of the rider who had just separated from the others. LA in person.

He smiled, just as the old man raised his voice.

"Doctor! Out.

Clay showed up at the door. The rifle, in hand, held under the armpit, point forward.

"Here, Amazee.

"Is my son in there?

"Yes, is here.

"I want to see it!

Come and see.

"I am not going to fall into a trap. Remove it. Let me see it.

Clay went into the house, picked up the boy, and led him to the door.

"Here it is, Amazee.

He had placed Tob's body before him.

"Has he been tied up? But... Son, are you okay?

"Answer, Tob.

"Yes father. Can't you get me out of here? These damn ...

Clay shoved the rifle into his kidneys.

"Shut up, asshole.

"Son, we're going to get you out now. You, doctor.

Clay shoved Tob away and tossed him into the room.

"What's up?

"Release my son.

"Amazee, don't get overheated. It could be very bad for you.

"Leave my health alone and... let go of the boy!

"Head for head, Amazee. I need Lane's.

"Why?

"You know it perfectly. And I'm going to tell you one thing: The slightest sign that your men want to do something against us will mean the death of your son. And I am not going to argue any more! Either you give me Lane, or you never see your son alive again. Have you understood? Lane has committed two crimes, and her son knew about them. Now it's up to you!

"Doctor, can I ...

"I said I don't want to argue anymore! Give me Lane! Bring it on!

There was a silence. Almost a minute.

"I don't know where Lane is. He is not with me.

"It's okay. I will kill the boy.

"Wait!

"To what?

"I listened...

The old man was panting. It showed in his voice. Clay frowned.

"I talked.

"If I turn Lane over to you, you...

"I will return your son to you. And God knows that I would like to kill him with my bare hands, because he is a pig, but I will keep my word.

"But if I don't have Lane ...

"Look it up!

He paused.

"You can do it. He has men and he has power. He has always abused both. Well ... use them! Get Lane.

"Doctor, can I come in?

"So that?

"To talk with you.

"Disarm yourself and come.

The old man dropped his weapons.

"Tell your men not to move from where they are. Let them not move for a single moment... except to search for Lane.

The old man turned and spoke. Clay listened. He repeated his words without adding anything.

Then Amazee entered.

"Pup, are you...?

He leaned over his son.

"Dad" said the young man, "can't you kill this ...?

"Shut up! I will fix the situation.

He turned to the group watching him: Clay, Sally, and Hough.

"I see" he said.

"What?

It was Clay. I was staring at him.

"I will not argue anymore. I just wanted to see if my son was... okay. Half is. I'm going to ignore him, because his life is worth more to me than that of a foreman. Terms?

He spoke serenely.

"My conditions are: Lane.

"His head?

"Not. Alive. I want to kill him myself.

"He'll get it.

"And... I'm not done. We will leave here with your son. We'll release it as soon as we're away.

"How will I know that they are not going to kill him?

"You will have to believe me, Amazee. It's a matter of take it or leave it.

"You," said the old man, laboriously, "are the first person to put me on the cross.

"It's not my business, Amazee. Do you accept or not? I do not want to argue.

"Is the life of a red skin so worth to you?

Sally put her hand on Clay's arm when she saw white lines of anger appear on Clay's face.

"It's okay. What is worth to me is something that is not enough for you. Not you, not many others like you. What is important is ... that now I have the strength and that is the only thing that you have understood in your life. The force! Hang on now, Amazee. Many times he has made others swallow it. Get it now! I could talk to you about human rights; I would not understand. But if we speak the same language, he will understand. Bring me Lane.

Amazee was watching him hypnotically.

"So, that's your position.

"Yes.

"He'll get it.

"You know where it is.

"I think so.

"Bring it.

"Here?

"Yes, damn it. Here.

"Doctor," said Hough, in a calm tone, "why don't you choose another place?"

Clay turned to him.

"Because I do not want to! Here I am where I can give orders. I want this place and no other. And the interests and principles of the Overseas can go to hell as far as I'm concerned.

"I suppose" said Amazee ", who knows that after what he has done to me he will not be able to go anywhere ...

He realized that he was about to threaten the man who had all the triumphs going for him, and he shut his mouth. Clay smiled.

"How come the sheriff didn't bring his little friend?

"I have wanted to solve this matter myself. I do not wish that ...

"Well. And now... Lane. You have to know where you are.

The old man went to the door. Once in it, he turned.

"Boy" he said to Tob ", don't worry. "And to Clay": You could have had what you would have wanted with me if you hadn't done this.

"Go to hell.

And the old man left. They saw him confer with his men and how they started walking.

"Now let's wait" said Clay.

"Doctor, you should..." Hough began. But he fell silent when he saw the other's expression ". And you, Sally ...

"I already know it. The Overseas will fire me.

"I have not said so much, but ...

"And I don't care, Hough. I would do it again.

"Yes, I know what kind of woman you are. Stubborn and... courageous. Doctor, what are you going to do when Lane is brought to you?

"What you don't know isn't going to hurt you, Hough.

"I understand.

Mac came down from the roof.

"Well, they are gone.

The afternoon passed slowly. At six o'clock, a group of horsemen arrived at the post. Hough came out to give them their instructions. There were five of them and they seemed determined and capable. They took care of everything in a moment, without asking questions when they saw those tied men, whose hands had only been untied in turn to give them food.

Clay watched Hough's calculating gaze. He could almost guess her thought. The Overseas inspector had thought for a moment about taking over the situation with his men, but seemed to give up.

They waited.

And the night came, and the night passed. Clay slept only a moment, while Mac watched. Then Sally took over. Dawn surprised them already up.

Almost just as the red disk peeked out from behind the mountains, they saw them.

"Clay" said Mac. I think they are coming.

"On the roof.

"This is already becoming a habit. Before long my ears will grow out and I will start meowing for food and drinking milk from a plate.

Old Amazee rode at the head of the group.

"Bester! Doctor!

Clay leaned out the door.

"Well?

"Here it is.

Two of his men stepped forward, leading another between them. His hands were tied to the pommel of the chair.

"Bring him over here.

"Let's go guys.

The two men approached the other. They left him almost by the door.

"Hi, Lane," Clay said softly.

The other raised his blue eyes. There was a strange expression about them.

Suddenly, he raised his voice.

"Amazee, you have sold me, Judas!

"It was about my son's life for yours, Lane.

"You have crucified me!

"You only crucified yourself when you did that with the Indian girl. When he killed her. When he hit Sally. You alone, Lane. Do not blame anyone.

"What are you going to do with me?

"What you didn't do with them. Give you a chance to draw the revolver at the same time as me.

"You want to assassinate me.

Clay shrugged.

"Take it as you like. At the moment, I don't care.

"Bester! Amazee howled. My son.

"I already told you. I'll take it. But I give you my word that I will return it to you safe and sound.

"You are going to give it to me right now!

"Not. I don't want him to fall on me with all those people. I'll take it.

And in a low voice:

"Sally, do you have things ready?

"Everything.

"Mac?

"Yes, Clay.

"Good, Amazee. You go back to your ranch. Your son will be joining you soon.

"You will not comply, what you say!

"I will fulfill it. And do not call me a liar again because it will weigh you down. Here, the only liars are you.

"Mr. Amazee, don't leave me alone with that guy," Lane said.

"I don't want to talk about that matter any more. Amazee, go back to your ranch or town, wherever you want. But ... get out!

The old man doubted. He ran his hand through his hair. Panting:

"Bester, if something happens to the boy, I swear I will chase him across the country, across the United States.

"I have already told you that nothing is going to happen to you. And now ... are they leaving or not?

There was still a slight hesitation. Then Amazee said:

"Guys, get going.

"Mr. Amazee!

It was Lane. His face was livid, of an unhealthy color.

"Don't leave me here, Mr. Amazee.

"Mac, let go of Mr. Amazee's men" he said.

Clay ". We don't need them. Just Tob and... my dear, my well-loved Lane.

Mac obeyed. The three men went to join the others.

And the whole group started slowly. Clay was targeting Lane with his rifle.

The tense scene lasted almost half an hour, until the group was lost on the horizon.

"Sure," said Hough, "they haven't left. They will surely wait for you anywhere, and they will surely make you pay dearly for all this. At least that's what I would do instead.

"And I" agreed Clay. But ... Mac.

"We are not going to indulge them. We will head to the mountains. In them, nobody will find me. I know them as if I was born into them.

Clay nodded.

"Sally" said Hough, "have you thought it through? You go?

She shook her head affirmatively.

"Yes, Hough" he said later. I'm going. I am sorry.

"No, I know you don't feel it. But at least I understand. Well, I wish you good luck.

"Wait a minute," Clay said.

Lane had made a move. Mac went to him.

"Don't move, you fucking pig. Do not move.

"Listen, I ...

Sally confronted him.

"Lane, have you lost your guts?

"Listen, Sally ...

"Not. You hit me, remember? You had me held by two men and you hit me with the belt.

Lane closed her mouth. His eyes seemed wild in their sockets.

"Hough" said Clay, suddenly ", would you like to witness a duel?

"A challenge? Do you want to fight with that man?

"I already told. But they think I'll do it far from here. No, by the way. I'm going to do it... here. In front of you. They will be my witnesses.

"Okay that," said Mac. Very good, yes, sir.

"Listen, doctor ...

"Do you or do you not want to serve as a witness? You and your men.

Hough shrugged.

"If you are determined ...

"I am.

"In that case, do what you want.

"Will you be a witness, if someone asks?

"I will be. My men and I will be.

"It will be murder," Lane said.

"Not. It will be a fight. Mac, prepare a pistol, with the whole load of bullets. Then you're going to unleash that guy. And, Sally, bring young Amazee. He also has the right to see it.

Hough's men had been drawing closer. In the eyes of all of them you could read that they would not miss this for the world.

"Hough, can you put yourself in the middle of the two" said Clay. You will be the referee.

"According.

Mac walked over to Lane. With a quick movement he cut the ropes that held him to the pommel of the chair.

"Come down, pig.

Lane dropped to the ground. He looked around.

"No, you cannot run away. What you can do is pray.

Mac had the revolver in one hand. The rifle in the other.

"Stay where you are, Lane.

Clay turned to Sally. She was looking at him, her face pale.

"Clay, for the love of God, be careful. I have heard that this man is left-handed and shoots ...

"Shut up. Do not worry. I have to do it, anyway.

She hugged him. Then he released it. Tob watched them.

"Lane! "He said". Kill him!

Clay hit him in the mouth, without much force.

"Shut up or after him you will go.

"You will remember.

"And you.

Then he howled:

"Mac! Can you give him the gun?

"As soon as you get ready.

Clay planted himself in the center of the courtyard. Hough walked until he was between them. Some of his men drew their pistols.

"No, guys, I don't think he's trying to shoot at me.

"Just in case, boss" said one of them.

And a moment later, the two men were alone in the center of the courtyard.

"Hough, count twenty yards between the two of you," Clay said.

Hough counted them slowly. He showed Lane where he could stand, and the other did.

Clay wiped his hands on the seat of his pants. Lane did the same. Then Mac walked up to him and looked at Clay.

"Already" said this one.

Mac grabbed the pistol by the butt.

"If you try to shoot before I say already, I'll kill you" he said, raising the rifle.

"Go to hell.

"Come on Mac," Clay said.

Sally closed her eyes for a moment. When he opened them again, the two men were facing each other. Hough, in the middle, away from the firing line.

Clay was calm. He was looking directly at his enemy, who, a little crouched, already had his pistol in his revolver, where Mac had placed it.

The sun was against Clay. This one realized a little late, but no longer wanted to change places. Hough saw it too. But if he caught the doctor's attention, he could be distracted and that would be fatal.

With his left hand, he pushed his hat forward. That move was about to lose him.

Lane put his hand to his left leg and the revolver leaped from it.

Clay followed suit. His hand seemed to be slower than usual, and then he leaned slightly down and to one side. That saved his life. The bullet, which would have hit his heart, grazed his arm. By then, he was already shooting.

Two of his bullets found Lane's body and spun him around violently, so that his other shots flew harmlessly into the air.

And Clay emptied his revolver on the body. The last bullet hit Lane already on the ground.

Clay straightened up. He was panting slightly. A thin trickle of blood ran down his arm.

Sally was running toward him.

"You are injured!

"No, it's just a scratch.

"Wait, I have to take your shirt off...

"Later.

Hough walked over to Lane and looked at him.

"Dead" he said.

Then he shook Clay's hand.

"I'm glad, doctor.

"Thanks.

He turned to Tob, who was staring at him, swallowing hard.

"Listen, Amazee. In a moment he can go. Walking.

"Walking?

"I have said it. Walking. I don't want him to catch up with his father until we're well away. But first I want to do something for you. Mac, untie it.

"What are you going to do with me? The same as...?

"No, just give him a beating that he remembers all his life.

Mac stared at Clay.

"Wait, Clay, wouldn't it be better if you just dropped it and...?

"Not. Untie it.

"As you like.

Did. Tob stretched his long limbs. A wary look appeared in his eyes.

"If I win ...

"If he beats me, Mac will let him go. Free. But...

Tob didn't wait. He jumped up and his fist came toward Clay's jaw. He smiled, turned his head away, and slammed his fist into Tob's liver.

Amazee's son doubled over on himself. Then Clay hit him with a jab to the chin and threw him back. Before he hit the ground, he landed two more punches. The young man's body fell to the ground.

Come on, get up.

Tob did. He had barely reached the vertical when Clay already rushed over him.

A hook, another side blow and... to the ground.

"Stand up.

But this time Tob didn't obey. He was bleeding from his mouth and from one eyebrow. One of his eyes was almost closed.

"Do not get up? Well, Hough, they have been witnesses. We are leaving. Let it go as soon as we are gone. Can I trust you?

"You can do it, doctor. And good luck.

He picked up Sally and put an arm around her shoulders.

"Good luck to you, girl.

Five minutes later they were outside the post, mounted on their horses and followed by the mules.

"You're going to let me go right now," Tob said to Hough.

"Really? Not until at least two hours have passed "the agent replied." You are not able to walk after the corrective you have been given.

"Damned...

Hough stared at him.

Listen, young man, I am not dependent on your father. I belong to the Overseas. And what is done at the post, I order it. Has understood? And if you were thinking of telling your father, remember one thing: There is a pending account between you and the Overseas, for assault and destruction of property and mistreatment of a post office employee. You will see what you prefer.

Tob closed his lips.

EPILOGUE

Dear Hough, Do you remember me? Just a few short letters to inform you that we found ... that is why so many people have always died. A yellow metal. Old Mac was right. The reef existed. And he has already denounced it and is working like a force to extract it. But there is and it is enough.

"You think I care? Well no. Clay and I will only take part of that gold. Long enough for Clay to set up an office in Tulsa. And no, it will be work that a good doctor like my husband is lacking. Because, you know, we were married two days ago.

"It would take a long time to tell what we went through until we made old Amazee lose our trail in the mountains. But we get it.

»We have achieved everything.

Even happiness, which is worth everything.

»Your most affectionate

"Sally."

END